WITH A VENGEANCE

ADAM CROFT

BLACK CANNON
PUBLISHING

First published in Great Britain in 2017.

This edition published in 2021 by Black Cannon Publishing.

ISBN: 978-1-912599-64-6

A CIP catalogue record for this book is available from the British Library.

Printed and bound in Great Britain by Clays Ltd, Elcograf S.p.A.

MORE BOOKS BY ADAM CROFT

RUTLAND CRIME SERIES

1. What Lies Beneath
2. On Borrowed Time
3. In Cold Blood

KNIGHT & CULVERHOUSE CRIME THRILLERS

1. Too Close for Comfort
2. Guilty as Sin
3. Jack Be Nimble
4. Rough Justice
5. In Too Deep
6. In The Name of the Father
7. With A Vengeance
8. Dead & Buried
9. In Too Deep
10. Snakes & Ladders

PSYCHOLOGICAL THRILLERS

- Her Last Tomorrow

- Only The Truth
- In Her Image
- Tell Me I'm Wrong
- The Perfect Lie
- Closer To You

KEMPSTON HARDWICK MYSTERIES

1. Exit Stage Left
2. The Westerlea House Mystery
3. Death Under the Sun
4. The Thirteenth Room
5. The Wrong Man

All titles are available to order from all good book shops.

Signed and personalised books available at adamcroft.net/shop

EBOOK-ONLY SHORT STORIES

- Gone
- The Harder They Fall
- Love You To Death
- The Defender

To find out more, visit adamcroft.net

1
ELEVEN YEARS AGO

The night was still. The four men held their breath. The loudest sound was the the pulse of blood in their own ears.

The back of the Transit van was dark but for the beam emanating from Footloose's torch. The other three watched as Footloose's hand signalled the countdown: five fingers, then four, three, two, one. With a nod, he turned and pushed open the rear doors of the van, the other three men following close behind.

Within seconds, they were inside the industrial unit. Their inside man had done his job and would be paid handsomely.

That was always the trickiest part of jobs like this — until it got to this moment, you never quite knew whether your man on the inside was stringing you along or not. They'd all heard of huge plans that had gone wrong because their contact had gone to the law or, worse, arranged to double-cross them. But this was all going perfectly to plan.

Once they were inside, Headache got to work on the on-duty security guard, pinning him to the ground before he'd managed to grab hold of his radio and sound the alarm.

The guard was a tough cookie. Much bigger than they'd been led to believe, but it only took Headache a few seconds to live up to his name, delivering a skull-splitting headbutt to the man's face, knocking him unconscious. With the guard now a little easier to manipulate, Headache and Bruno frisked him down, removing his tools and equipment, before gagging him and handcuffing him to the copper pipework.

'Oi, Footloose. We've got a problem here!' Peter yelled from inside the office. They only ever used their nicknames when on a job. They couldn't risk blowing their real identities, and they never knew who was listening.

'What do you mean "problem"?' Footloose replied, seemingly unruffled. Despite the calm tone of his voice, Headache and Bruno knew when Footloose was upset. Their years of knowing him and working with him meant they would realise a couple of seconds before most people. That still wouldn't give them enough time to get out of his way, though.

Footloose walked through to the office and looked down at Peter, who was crouched down by the safe.

'It's not the model he told us it was,' Peter said. 'I'm not tooled up for this one.'

Footloose looked him in the eye and spoke calmly. 'What do you mean you're not tooled up?'

'I mean, this needs extra gear. I can't get into this with the tools I've brought. I'm going to need—'

Peter's sentence was cut short by Footloose lifting him up by the front of his overalls and pinning him to the wall. He could hear the fabric ripping and tearing as it struggled to hold his weight, his feet dangling a good few inches off the ground.

'You're a bloody safe breaker,' Footloose yelled, spittle flying through the mere millimetres that separated their faces. He pulled Peter away from the wall and slammed him back against it with each word. 'You. Break. Safes. Get it?'

Before Peter could reply, Footloose's attention was taken by the distant sound of sirens.

'Footloose! There's sirens!' Bruno called from outside the office.

'I can hear that,' came the reply, as he threw Peter to the ground. 'Now what the fuck's going on?'

He could see immediately that none of the others had any clue.

'They're getting closer. They're coming here!' Bruno said.

Footloose knew he had to make his decision quickly.

'We need to split. Headache, back out the way we came. You too, you useless prick,' he said through gritted teeth, picking Peter up and shoving him over towards Headache. 'Bruno, with me. We'll take the fire escape.'

The men nodded and made to do as they were told, before Footloose gave them one last instruction.

'And remember. If there's even the slightest possibility that anyone's following you to the safe house — even the tiniest fraction of a chance — you abandon. Alright?'

The men nodded again, and Footloose gestured for them to get moving.

It took three shoulder-barges for Bruno to shake the back door free of its hinges, before he and Footloose clambered up the metal stairs, jumped the low wall and ran off into the woods behind the industrial estate.

Towards the front of the unit, Peter and Headache were ready to break for the exit. As they rounded the corner and started to run towards the van, their attention was taken by a voice shouting from the darkness. Peter carried straight on to the van, but Headache stopped and turned towards the voice.

A man jogged out of the shadows, clearly almost out of breath, his policeman's uniform reflecting under the streetlights.

'Get on the floor,' the policeman said, struggling to talk between breaths. 'Get down. Hands behind your head.'

'Yeah, as if,' Headache replied, turning to join Peter back at the van before the rest of the cops arrived. He could see this guy had no weapons, no truncheon, nothing. Just a beat cop who'd heard the call go out over the radio and been unlucky enough to get here first.

'Wait,' the policeman called out. 'I know you. Don't I?'

'Headache! Get in the van!'

Headache looked at the policeman for a moment. 'No. Sorry. You're mistaken.'

'Yeah I do. You're—'

'Headache! Now!'

'Yeah. Last September. The Moulson Arms. I know who you are.'

'Headache! I'm going if you don't get in the van right now!'

Headache's jaw started to tense as he stretched out his hand, then quickly dipped it into his inside jacket pocket, pulled out the Makarov pistol and raised it in front of him, the barrel pointed directly at the policeman's head.

'Jesus Christ, Headache! No!' Peter yelled, by now revving the van's engine and beeping the horn to get his attention.

Headache swallowed, narrowed his eyes, and pulled the trigger.

2
PRESENT DAY

Freddie Galloway took the stairs two at a time, the thick black smoke filling his lungs. Even though his joints were telling him to take it easy, his mind was alive and his heart was pumping, telling him he had to get out of here – quickly.

He didn't want to die by being choked to death by the smoke, nor did he want the flames to take him. He'd worked hard enough his whole life, been shat on from the start, and he wasn't about to succumb like this. The one thing he'd always had was control, and he wasn't going to give that up now.

He reached the top of the stairs and crossed the wide landing, before closing his bedroom door behind him. The fire was coming from the front of the house, leaving him with very few options. He paused and turned for a moment, watching the smoke starting to billow under the door and rise, dispersing to fill the room with a thick haze.

It wouldn't be long. He could see the light changing underneath the door. The fire had already begun to climb the stairs and it wouldn't be long before it would consume the bedroom door, the flames licking underneath it, blackening the wood.

He blinked, and immediately his eyes reverted back to what was in front of him: billowing smoke, and plenty of it.

The heat was becoming unbearable. If he was going to get out of here, it wasn't going to be back through the bedroom door: the fire was now too close and the door had begun to radiate immense amounts of heat. He swore he could see the colour of the wood beginning to change as it was charred from behind.

Almost as if he hadn't noticed it up until now, he started to become aware of the sound of the fire. Not just the crackling and snapping of his prized possessions succumbing to the flames, but the vast roar of the inferno as it consumed every available molecule of oxygen in the building.

And it was a big building. Freddie Galloway had worked hard all his life. He wasn't a grafter in the conventional sense, but at least he'd worked hard at working smart. He knew a lot of people who'd spent their whole lives doing twelve-hour days and who were now struggling to get by on the state pension. You couldn't expect anyone to do anything for you in this life. Freddie had learnt that early on.

He had always been proud to tell people he was a stubborn bastard. He made no bones about it. It was what had got him where he was, he'd say. Business was no place for faint hearts. Real men made decisions, and they stuck to them.

Without thinking twice, Freddie hobbled over to the french windows on the far side of the bedroom and flung them open. Immediately, he could hear the fire roaring behind him, gulping down this fresh, pure oxygen that had just been let into the furnace.

With the flames now rising up the inside of the door, Freddie knew he had to act fast. Grunting and groaning, he pulled one of his wicker chairs across the tiled balcony and climbed up onto it, his head giddy with the smoke as he peered over the edge of the railings and down onto the grounds of his house below. The fire had started at the front of the house, and looking down now it would be hard to believe there was a fire at all. The patio furniture stood gleaming in the moonlight, the cool, still swimming pool reflecting the profile of the house he'd worked so hard for.

He knew he couldn't give his decision another thought. This wasn't about to be the first decision Freddie Galloway would regret in his long, tough life. The pool was reaching up to him. Unsteady on his feet, he clambered up onto the railings and swung his legs over them, holding on with shaking arms. Pushing his feet off the edge of the balcony, he took one last breath before jumping, watching the image of his falling body reflected in the pool below.

3

The overriding thought going through Detective Sergeant Wendy Knight's mind was that she'd hoped she'd seen the back of these Blackstone's manuals. The police guidance books were heavy going, and it was at times like this she wondered if a more laid-back career might be good for her.

Deep down, though, she knew she was kidding herself. She could've thrown the copies of Blackstone's away after becoming a Sergeant, or at any time since, but she'd kept them around for a reason. Probably the same reason she'd kept all the updated guidance that had been issued from above, spiral bound and stored away in her spare bedroom ready for future reference. Because she'd always known, always hoped, that there'd be a need for future reference.

She wasn't afraid to admit that the first feeling that crossed her mind when DCI Culverhouse had suggested she go for her inspectors' exams was overwhelming pressure. At first she thought it was the fear of failure, of having to go through all this extra effort at a time when they were already overworked and understaffed. But she had gradually come to realise that she wasn't afraid of failing. She was afraid of succeeding.

Reaching the rank of Detective Inspector would mean she'd have achieved the same level of career progression as her father, DI Bill Knight, before he'd been cruelly taken far too young, trying to intercept a bungled robbery whilst off duty. Achieving parity with her father, the great man that he'd been, felt to Wendy as though she was betraying him. And knowing that DCI Jack Culverhouse was quite likely grooming her as his eventual successor as Detective Chief Inspector would mean she'd ultimately outrank her father — if she chose to do so, that was.

Many times, people had tried to tell her that she couldn't let her father rule her career from beyond the grave. They told her Bill Knight would have been proud of her, would have wanted her to go far beyond what he'd managed to achieve in his own career. But that didn't mean it felt any less wrong to Wendy.

It had always felt grossly unfair that her father's career and life had been cut short. Of course it did. But it felt somehow perverse that she should be able to achieve a higher rank than he did purely because she'd been fortunate enough not to die young.

That said, she knew what her father's response would've been. It would have been the same as her mother's. They both would have told her to go for it, said they were proud of her and would've given her all the support she needed – and more.

She poured herself another glass of wine and sat back for a moment. If she were to become a Detective Inspector, it would change her life and her career quite significantly. Apart from the pay rise of almost ten grand a year after a couple of years in the job, it would mean more responsibility and more time spent at work. She was already wedded to the job, though, and she saw no reason not to do even more. After all, it wasn't as though she had much of a personal life to write home about. No partner, no family – other than a brother banged up in prison – and no real prospect of any of that changing any time soon.

If she didn't pass the exam, she'd have to wait another year to take it again. Culverhouse, though, seemed confident. He'd already started giving Wendy more responsibility, as if priming her for becoming a DI. As far as Wendy was concerned, nothing was a foregone conclusion. There would be up to one hundred and twenty questions from across the board in policing terms, and that was a hell of a lot to swot up on. She'd always kept across things in general, but then again it had been a long time since she was tested on it in an exam situation.

She took a swig of wine and lay down on her side on the sofa, spooning her cat, who was curled up on the cushion next to her.

'What do you reckon, Cookie? Think I should just forget the whole thing and enjoy the small amount of time I do get off work? You'd like that, wouldn't you?'

Cookie buried his head further into the cushion and pressed himself against Wendy, as if answering her question.

'Yeah. Well, maybe we'll just have to work our cuddle sessions around paperwork and personal progress meetings. Or we'll wait for Bring Your Cat To Work Day. You'd like that. You could eat all the bits of bacon sandwich Steve drops on the floor.'

Detective Sergeant Steve Wing, one of Wendy's colleagues at Mildenheath CID, had something of a reputation for not being the fittest or tidiest of the team.

She kissed Cookie on the head and sat up again.

'You don't really care unless you get fed, do you? Sometimes I think life would be a lot easier if I was a cat.'

Wendy had got used to living alone. She'd done so for years, and there'd never been any sign on the horizon of it being otherwise, other than an ill-fated romance with a local accountant, Robert Ludford. That had ended in tragedy and heartache, with both her lover and her unborn child losing their lives within a short period of time.

If she was completely true to herself, she had hoped a relationship with Xav might have been on the cards, but that had very definitely been halted in its tracks recently.

Wendy and Xavier Moreno, a civilian IT expert from police headquarters at Milton House, had been attempting to develop a relationship for quite some time. After ending up sleeping together following too much wine one night at Wendy's, they'd tried to do things properly — dates, restaurants and everything. But, as it always did, work had got in the way on more than one occasion and Wendy had let Xav down. They'd barely spoken in a couple of months, and she'd thought things had been left on bad terms.

She took another swig of wine and went to reach for the bottle to give herself a top-up, but stopped when she noticed her mobile phone vibrating on the coffee table. The screen showed Jack Culverhouse's name as it danced across the surface. Why was he calling her at this time of the evening? She wasn't on call tonight. That didn't tend to mean much at all, though. When Jack Culverhouse wanted you on his team, you didn't have any other options. Being as short-staffed as Mildenheath CID was, they were generally fine to rotate their on-call hours, but when a major case came in it was all hands to the pump. This, then, could only mean one thing.

Wendy took a deep breath and answered the call.

4

Jack Culverhouse always did a great job of looking pissed off when his downtime had been disturbed by virtue of being the on-call DCI when a new case came in, but in reality he was pleased to have the distraction. His personal life certainly wasn't boring or empty. Quite the opposite. It was a car crash.

Once again, Emily would likely wake up and find her dad gone, back into work again for another case. He wondered how long he could carry on doing this. He'd already lost her once, his wife taking off with her when Emily was a toddler, citing Jack's obsession with work as her reason for leaving. Although Emily was now in her teenage years and seemed much more forgiving of his lifestyle than her mother had been, there was a definite underlying anger that he needed to help heal.

He poured the hot water from the kettle onto the

instant coffee granules, then added some cold water from the tap. He was going to have to drink it quickly.

'Knight. We've got a juicy one. Fire over at Little Walgrave. Arson, they reckon. Just had the call to confirm. It's closer to yours, so get your skates on and I'll meet you over there. I'll be a few minutes behind.'

He heard Wendy sigh as he took a swig of coffee. 'I'm not on call. Do you really need to be bringing people into the office for an arson? The duty team can deal with that.'

'I wish it could,' Culverhouse replied, knowing that the Chief Constable, Charles Hawes, would be even more mindful of budget restrictions and overtime bills than anyone, 'but that's not the full picture. It's a residential address.'

He could almost hear Wendy looking up at her clock, noticing the time and realising what that meant.

'Shit. Are there bodies?'

'I don't know. It's not clear yet. It's still early days so I don't think they know what's gone on. All the fire chief said was that it was immediately obvious it was an arson attack. No possibility of an accident. So either way we've got a crime scene. But apparently one of the neighbours came over and told them there was one guy living there on his own. At this time of night, I imagine he would've been in there, yeah.'

In cases of arson, it was always vital that the police acted quickly. Often, arsonists would either hang around or return to the scene to watch their work in action. You could almost set your clock by it. And with fire, the great destroyer, actively attempting to eradicate the evidence, it was crucial that the emergency services worked together to salvage what they could and act whilst the scene was fresh.

He heard Wendy sigh from the other end of the phone. 'Can you pick me up at least? I've had a drink. Only had a glass or so, but I'm not going to risk it.'

Culverhouse shook his head, knowing she couldn't see him. Back in his day, there would have been no doubt about a CID officer dropping everything to attend the scene of a crime. There was a passion, a hunger to get justice at all costs. Nowadays that'd all been eaten away by red tape and bureaucracy. Had it been him twenty years ago, he would've jumped in a cab – hell, he would've sprinted over hot coals – if it meant getting to the scene and starting to oil the wheels of justice. Now, though, things were different. There were budget cuts and Working Time Directives. Jack Culverhouse didn't give a shit about any of that. All he wanted was to catch the people responsible for the crimes that plagued Mildenheath. And he was still willing to do that at all costs.

'Right. Well get your fucking shoes on and wait on the road. I'm not sitting in the car while you fanny around with your high heels.'

Jack Culverhouse ended the call, put his phone back in his pocket and downed the rest of the mug of coffee.

It was going to be a long night.

5

Culverhouse's car swept past the cordon and up the long driveway as Wendy looked out at the house in front of them. Although it had been largely gutted by the inferno, which the fire officers were still trying to put out, she could see that it had clearly been a huge, very impressive building.

It was all clad in white — most of which had now turned to black — and Wendy reckoned the front face of the house must have a good dozen or so windows. What was left of them, at least.

There was a large burgundy red car on the driveway. A Bentley, she thought, although she didn't usually pay much attention to cars. She could certainly admire the sleek curves and style of this model, though — if she had been made of money. There wouldn't be much left of this car very shortly. Even from a distance, she could already see the paintwork starting to blister and bubble from the heat, and the windows closest to the house were blackened.

Whoever owned this house was not only a very wealthy individual, but had clearly done something to upset somebody. Wendy was no expert on fire damage, but she doubted whether anything would be left of the house once they'd put out the flames.

Although they'd already made good progress up the driveway, they were stopped at a cordon a good fifty yards away by the Watch Commander, who introduced himself as Matthew Leeman.

'This is one of the most blatant arson attacks I've seen,' he said, shaking Jack and Wendy's hands. 'We can't get any closer at the moment, but you can smell the accelerant from here. We'll know more once the blaze has died down, but it looks to me as though the core is at the front of the house, by the front door.'

Wendy had to admit that she couldn't smell anything other than the smoke that occasionally drifted over, but deferred to Leeman's greater knowledge and experience.

'How long do you think it'll take to put it out?'

Leeman shrugged. 'Impossible to say. House fires don't usually take too long, but this is a big house. And whatever's in there, it's burning well. Whoever started this fire wanted to make damn sure it did as much damage as possible.'

'Not kids then?' Culverhouse asked.

'I wouldn't say so. It's not my job to come up with a list of suspects, but it doesn't look like kids messing about to me. Whoever did it would've had to come all the way up the driveway, risk being seen doing it, pour God knows how much accelerant through the letterbox and get away without anyone seeing them. Kids set fire to fly-tips and old sheds, not bloody great mansions.'

'Has there been anyone hanging around?'

'Not that we've noticed. Although you could easily hide away in the trees over there without being seen. Thermal imaging might help.'

Culverhouse snorted. 'Yeah, I don't think there's much chance of me being given authorisation to put a chopper in the air though, do you?'

The police helicopter equipped with thermal imaging equipment would cost a couple of thousand pounds an hour just to put it in the air, and policing budgets were already extremely tight.

'Plus you've got the fire throwing out all sorts of heat,' Wendy offered. 'We should at least ask, though. They can only say no.'

'I'll ring it through. Can't see it doing much good, though,' Culverhouse grunted.

While Culverhouse walked off to make the call, Wendy thought it would be a good opportunity to ask the Watch Commander some more questions. She'd never attended an arson attack before — not something like this, anyway. She'd been called out to small fires in garages when she was a uniformed PC, but this was something entirely different. Besides which, there was nothing either of them could do at this stage apart from watch the fire crews tackle the blaze.

'How much of your job's actually taken up fighting fires then?' she asked.

'Not much of it, thankfully. Although you always remember it when you do. Most of it's about drills, training exercises, talks in schools, risk assessments, paperwork...'

Wendy chuckled. 'Sounds familiar.'

'Plus we're now paramedics, apparently,' Leeman jibed, referring to the fact that the current UK government had suggested that fire officers be given extra medical training so they could double as paramedics, allowing politicians to cut the NHS budget even further.

'I know the feeling. Wouldn't ever think of doing another job, though, eh?'

'Oh I'm tempted sometimes, don't you worry. But no. I don't think anything else would give me the variety, unpredictability and levels of addictive stress the fire service gives me.'

'Maybe you should try the police,' Wendy said, only half-joking.

A couple of minutes later, Culverhouse returned.

'The Chief Constable's wife must've been feeling fruity last night. He's just given authority to put Hotel Oscar Nine Nine in the air. Christ knows how long that'll be, though.'

Remarkably, the county didn't have its own police helicopter. Up until recently the force had its own chopper, but the introduction of the National Police Air Service in 2012 meant that many helicopter bases were closed. The county had agreed to close its own at a local RAF base on the understanding that its air support would then be provided under NPAS by the Metropolitan Police in London, only to later discover that the Met had rejected NPAS and continued to operate its own air support service. As a result, incidents given air support had dropped by up to 90% in some areas. Regardless, many officers still referred to the service by the previous force helicopter's call-sign.

'And in the meantime?' Wendy asked, both of Culverhouse and Leeman.

'In the meantime,' Leeman replied, 'we wait.'

6

In the early hours of the morning, the team began to assemble in the incident room for Culverhouse's first briefing on the case. There would be further briefings in which the members of the team kept everyone else updated on progress in their particular areas of investigation, but these were far less regular than they'd be in any other CID incident room.

The Mildenheath CID team was much smaller than others, and it also had the added advantage of being a good twenty miles from the county's main CID offices at Milton House – a purpose-built concrete and glass monstrosity towards the north of the county. Being in charge of a small, satellite CID unit suited Jack Culverhouse down to the ground. It meant he could, largely, do things his own way.

'Right. First incident room briefing for Operation Mandible, yada yada. People assembled et cetera et cetera. I'm DCI wassisface, you're all minions. Got it?'

Culverhouse often found his disdain for process and bureaucracy difficult to hide, and at times of increased pressure that tended to make itself known even more so than usual.

'We're looking at a serious case of arson on a residential property in Little Walgrave. There may or may not be casualties. To be honest, the house is massive and the fire's going to take a little while to put out. Never seen anything like it in my life. The fire officers won't let us anywhere near it until they've made everything safe, and that could be a while yet. They reckon they're starting to bring it under control, but whoever did this definitely wanted to make sure the whole place would be razed to the ground. It looks like they might have managed it, too.'

Culverhouse looked at Wendy, as if signalling that she should talk. *Nice of him to warn me*, she thought.

'Yes. Well, the fire officers seemed pretty certain that this was a deliberate act of arson,' Wendy said, standing. 'So once we know a bit more about who owns the property we can start to look at reasons why someone might have wanted to do them harm. I'm not sure if we'll be able to do that before morning, though. The house is pretty isolated. No neighbours nearby – closest house is about a hundred and fifty yards away – so at this stage everything is still pretty unknown. We should start to find all that out soon enough, but at the moment the focus is on letting them put out the fire, so everything else is a bit up in the air.'

'So why have we all been called in at stupid o'clock?' Detective Sergeant Frank Vine asked.

Culverhouse gave him an icy stare that told Frank everything he needed to know.

'In the meantime, I think we need to sit tight,' Wendy said, trying to defuse the tension. 'We can identify the homeowner from land registry records and we should get out and speak to any neighbours, too, even if they are hundreds of yards away. Someone'll know who lives in that house and we can start to get ahead of ourselves a bit. PNC checks, known issues in their lives. You know the drill.' The Police National Computer was often invaluable in finding out information about a person, should any police force in Britain have encountered them in the past.

Wendy had recently started to get more of an inkling of the pressures that were put on senior investigating officers from above. She knew Culverhouse wouldn't be in the team's good books for getting them up during the night when there wasn't a whole lot they could do at this stage, but she also knew that the Police and Crime Commissioner would have Culverhouse's guts for garters if he'd failed to react quickly and there were lives at stake.

The elected PCC, Martin Cummings, wasn't Culverhouse's biggest fan. The feeling was mutual. As far as Culverhouse was concerned, politics and policing didn't mix, but unfortunately for him the government disagreed.

'I'll be keeping in touch with the bloke in charge at the scene,' Culverhouse said. 'He'll be updating me regularly, and I'll pass on those updates to you. But in the meantime there's plenty we can be getting on with. If you're really stuck, Frank, feel free to clean my office.'

Culverhouse gave Frank Vine another icy stare and headed into said office. Detective Constable Debbie Weston gave him a few seconds, then followed.

'Guv, I was just wondering if I might be able to have a quick chat,' she said, hovering by the doorway.

'By all means.'

Debbie closed the door behind her. 'I was hoping to speak to you over the next couple of days anyway, but seeing as we're here, and as it's the calm before the storm...'

Culverhouse folded his arms and leaned forward on his desk. 'Spit it out, will you?'

'Well, the thing is, my mum's really not well. She's been in the home for a few years now but she's recently started to take a turn for the worse. I've been getting down there as much as I can, but it's a good couple of hours each way and squeezing it in between shifts just isn't feasible.'

'Right. So what are you trying to say?'

Debbie sighed. 'I'm trying to say would it be possible to request a temporary transfer — a secondment — to a force closer to her? Just so I can see her as much as possible. To be honest, it might not be for long.'

Culverhouse could see from the look in Debbie's eyes that this was upsetting her. She'd been the most stable and valuable member of his team for as long as he could remember, and had never had ambitions to become a sergeant. She'd been quite happy to get the work done to the best of her ability, and she'd proved to be the catalyst that unlocked an investigation on more than one occasion. She was, quite simply, his steadiest foot-soldier.

'It's not quite as easy as that,' he replied, stuck between genuinely wanting to help Debbie and not wanting to lose her – even temporarily. Besides which, a few weeks working on the south coast would probably make her change her mind about coming back to Mildenheath. He wouldn't blame her. 'I could ask, but there are no guarantees. Far from it. An operational secondment would be one thing, but there aren't any operational reasons to send you down to the south coast.'

Had Debbie been less loyal and more driven by career progression, there would have been a possibility of being sent on secondment to use her specialist skills. But on this occasion her modesty had been to her detriment.

'I know, but I thought perhaps there might be something on compassionate grounds. If not, I completely understand,' she said. 'I mean, I guess I could use up some of my leave. Even if it's unpaid. I could stay in a hotel down there and—'

'On a Detective Constable's salary? With a mortgage and bills to cover?'

'It might not be for long,' Debbie said quietly, the subtext clear to both of them.

'Look, I'll bend a few ears and see what I can do, alright? But there's definitely no promises.'

Debbie smiled. 'It's just that... Being so far away, I feel...'

She got no further, before breaking down in tears in front of the DCI. Culverhouse, in his usual style, had no idea how to deal with this. Interpersonal skills really weren't his bag.

'Listen,' he said. 'Why don't you take some time off? We'll call it sick leave, yeah? Just take a couple of days to get your head straight. Pop down and see your mum if you want.'

'But the new case...'

'Forget it. We'll sort it. Besides which, you're not much use to me sitting here blubbering away.'

Debbie allowed a slight laugh to break through the tears, recognising that Culverhouse was at least attempting to be sympathetic.

'I'll need you to get through today if you can. It's still early days on the case and we don't want anyone getting wind of you leaving after you've only been here an hour. Tomorrow morning I'll say you rang in with the shits or something.'

Debbie chuckled again. 'Thanks, guv. I won't let you down.'

7

'Told you this was pointless,' Frank Vine announced to no-one in particular as he huffed and puffed and sat back in his chair. 'Bloody Land Registry's website is down for maintenance and there's no-one on the phones until eight o'clock.'

Frank had been threatening retirement for a few years now, but had never actually gone through with it. He'd recently started making more noises about it to Culverhouse but the DCI knew that Frank was a creature of habit, and that retiring and moving away was probably just a pipe dream for him. Besides which, the amount of work he actually contributed was more or less akin to him not being there anyway.

'Nothing on the PNC?' DS Steve Wing asked. If the address had been linked with any investigations or reports of crimes in the past, the Police National Computer would have records linked to it, which would undoubtedly give some background information on the homeowner's name and particulars.

'Nope. We're gonna have to sit and wait it out. Which makes me wonder why we couldn't have done that at home,' Frank replied, directing his comment to Steve and giving a knowing look in the direction of DC Ryan Mackenzie, a relative newcomer to the team who had already gained a reputation for doing things completely by the book. She had joined the team fairly recently, and had made a strong impression from the start – particularly as Culverhouse had only seen her name and expected a new male officer.

'Don't look at me,' Ryan replied. 'I don't think any of us are particularly jumping for joy. Especially not me. I'm due to go off call at nine, and I've got a date night planned with Mandy.'

'Here's a question,' Steve started. From the other side of the office, Wendy had a feeling she knew what was coming next. 'What do you lot actually do? I mean, y'know. When you're getting down to it. I mean, there's nothing to put in, is there?'

'"Put in"? My, Steve, you put it so delicately. It's a wonder you're still single,' Ryan jabbed.

'No, what I actually mean is... Well, the gays, I can sort of see what they do. I get that. But your lot, that doesn't make sense. I mean, do you just sort of...' Steve trailed off, making clumsy conjoined scissoring actions with his fingers.

'Yeah. Something like that,' Ryan replied, sharing a pitying glance with Wendy.

'Still no word from the scene?' Steve asked Frank,

aware that he should probably change the topic of conversation.

'I know as much as you do. Probably still playing with their hoses,' Frank replied, giving Steve a good minute or so of chuckling at the weak innuendo.

While Steve was chuckling to himself, Debbie Weston left Culverhouse's office and returned to her desk.

'Here, what was that all about?' Steve asked. 'Not asking for a pay rise, I hope.'

'No, just a partition wall around my desk so I don't have to listen to your crap or watch you flick bits of sausage roll off your jumper all day,' Debbie replied, being met with a chorus of *Ooooh!*'s from Steve and Frank.

'Bloody hell. Been saving that one up, have you? Never had you down as joining in with office banter.'

'When did bullying become "banter", exactly, Steve?' Ryan chipped in. 'I've always wondered that.'

'Bullying? I only said was she asking for a bleedin' pay rise. That's bullying now, is it?'

'I'm talking about all the other times you decide to make snide comments. I know you're trying to be funny and impress your little mate over there, but maybe you should learn some actual jokes rather than resorting to picking on people.'

'I'll have you know I'm a Detective Sergeant and you're a Detective Constable,' Steve said.

'And I'm about to send an email reporting you for workplace bullying,' Ryan replied. 'So if I were you I'd get back to your sergeant's duties. Whatever they are.'

Wendy, Frank and Debbie tried to stifle their laughter as Steve slunk off back to his desk.

Wendy answered the ringing phone on her desk. It was the station duty office, otherwise known to punters as the front desk.

'We've got Mrs Wilson here,' the caller told her. 'Something about a vice den being set up in the house across the road. Drugs, prostitutes, the lot apparently. She reckons she's seen foreign dignitaries and members of the royal family popping in and out, smacked off their tits on heroin.'

Mrs Wilson had something of a reputation at Mildenheath Police Station. She was a rather sweet old lady who lived on the outskirts of town, but she was undoubtedly mad. She'd be in at least once a week, with some outlandish theory of hers which absolutely required a full CID response, as far as she was concerned. She'd been living on her own for years, and clearly relished the drama.

It was usually the case that a CID officer would go downstairs, take a very brief statement, reassure her they'd look into it, then come back upstairs and chuck it in the bin. It was a common misconception that all reported crimes had to be investigated.

'Steve? Time to earn your dignity back,' Wendy called out. 'Mrs Wilson's in reception for you.'

Wendy watched as Steve's body language told her everything. He closed his eyes, dropped his shoulders and sullenly left the major incident room, heading towards the station duty office.

Seconds later, Culverhouse's office door flew open and he came marching out into the middle of the room.

'Right. Listen up, you lot. I've just had Trumpton on the phone. The chopper found nothing, believe it or not. The only heat sources were from the fire itself and the crew attending the scene. Nothing in the surrounding woods at all, apart from the odd badger. They've managed to keep the fire down enough to get round the back of the house now, and they've found something a bit juicy. A dead body, to be precise. Good job you came in, isn't it?'

'What, in the house?' Wendy asked.

'Nope. On the back patio. Fallen from height, apparently. Probably to escape the fire. Inches away from the safety of the swimming pool, poor bastard. But here's the juicy bit. The body was the homeowner and the only person who lived there — one Mr Frederick Galloway. Ring any bells?'

'Freddie Galloway?' Frank asked. '*The* Freddie Galloway?'

'Got it in one, Frank. And it looks like his change of career from armed robbery to bungee jumping didn't go down too well.'

8

Benjamin Newell fumbled with his mobile phone to try and silence the alarm. He should've turned it off earlier: he'd been awake for the past three hours anyway.

He'd had a lot to think about. Today was to be a huge turning point in his life. The day he would finally put his past behind him and be able to focus on his new future as a married man.

Lisa had changed him — there was no doubt about that. She'd been good to him. She'd known about his past and had been forgiving enough to stick with him, to give him the chance to prove that he'd changed. She certainly wasn't the sort of woman who'd put up with having a husband embroiled in a life of crime. She couldn't risk that.

As a school teacher, she'd already been required to respond to a government questionnaire on whether she or anyone living in her house had a criminal record. If she'd lied, she would've been fired on the spot. If she'd answered truthfully, she knew she'd be suspended immediately while they investigated the circumstances. Even if someone living in your house — a parent, partner or friend — had once got into a drunken brawl thirty years earlier, it made no difference if you'd since become a priest or even a monk. You were a danger to the children, according to the Department for Education. The children you'd never meet because you weren't actually a teacher yourself — you just had the misfortune to live in the same house as one. Because, of course, it's a well-known fact that you can catch The Criminal Disease by breathing the same air as someone who once got done for having a punch up in a pub.

What had made Benjamin love Lisa even more was that she'd never even considered lying on the questionnaire. She knew she'd be up before the board of governors and would have to answer for herself — whatever the hell that meant — when it was revealed that her husband-to-be had a less than angelic background. But she didn't care. She was honest, upstanding and did things by the book. He'd just hoped she wouldn't suffer because of it. As it was, things all blew over very quickly and she was allowed to continue teaching. Probably something to do with the same government's policies and treatment of teachers resulting in an all-time record low number of new teachers coming through, causing a national shortage. Ironically, it probably wouldn't be long before they'd have to consider recruiting ex-cons just to get the kids through their school years.

He'd been lying in bed for the past three hours, staring at the ceiling. He knew every crack, every tiny fissure in the plaster. It was as if the spare bedroom was his, even though he'd never set foot in it before he'd come to his best man Cameron Morley's house last night.

It was now a few minutes past eight. He'd have to get up and get ready, make himself look presentable for his big day. And what a huge day it was.

He'd always wanted to get married, settle down and have kids. Alright, so the latter was unlikely to happen now, but you never knew. Lisa already had Aiden and Caitlin from her previous marriage, and she'd intimated that she wasn't exactly keen to start again – not now that Caitlin, the youngest, had turned nine only a couple of months earlier. But still, all he'd ever wanted was that stability – the loving family unit he'd never had when he was younger. He didn't care that the kids weren't his; he was going to love them all the same.

His parents had never been married. He'd thought that was a shame. It was also a fucking pain in the arse, as the other kids at school would use it as a way of getting at him. The bullying had only lasted a couple of years, though, until he'd managed to pick up a set of skills and a reputation at the school which meant he was no longer the target of bullies. After all, if you were the one who was able to pick open the lockers and go through other kids' stuff whenever you wanted, people tended to be nice to you.

Those early lock-picking days were a revelation to Benjamin. It had given his life a purpose. It had made him someone. He was the guy who picked locks. He'd spend his evenings and weekends trying different techniques to get into a variety of increasingly difficult locks (anything to get away from the noise of his parents arguing and smacking seven shades of shit out of each other) until he was breaking into cars and, eventually, safes.

At that point, this wasn't just a fun hobby or a harmless prank he'd play. It had become serious criminality. And the saddest thing was he didn't know where he'd crossed the line. It had sort of blurred, until one day he'd woken up and realised he'd become a major criminal. It was something he'd fallen into without even knowing about it. It was a familiar story — that much he knew from his time inside.

Unlike many other people he knew at that time, he'd only needed to be caught once. That was the wakeup call that told him he needed to change his ways, needed a new focus. And since meeting Lisa he'd had purpose in his life. He had something to live for. It was no longer a case of following the path of incidental self-destruction. He had ambitions and targets.

If he was true to himself, being caught hadn't been the wakeup call. That had come only a short while earlier, when the gunshot had rung out and he knew instantly that his life had changed forever, that there was no way back. Because there was never any coming back from that, whether you got caught or not. It was something that would live with you forever.

But, c'est la vie, he'd been caught and he'd done his time. No-one could argue with that. Sure, there were people who believed that a leopard never changes its spots, but one thing Benjamin had learnt was that there was always a gobby cunt with an opinion. Prison was there to reform and rehabilitate, and it had certainly worked as far as he was concerned.

He got up out of bed, looked at himself in the mirror and smiled. Today, he was going to make Lisa proud. He was going to show her just how right she'd been to stick with him after finding out about his past. He was going to repay her faith in spades. She would never have to want for anything again.

Tucking the crisp white shirt into the grey trousers, he did up the top button on his collar and tied the cravat in the way he'd seen done on the YouTube tutorials. Oh yes. A bit of gel in his hair and he'd look just the ticket. The husband. The step-father. The good man.

This was the first day of the rest of his life. And he was going to make it count.

9

The scene at Little Walgrave was much calmer when Jack Culverhouse and Wendy Knight returned later that morning. The sun had started to rise and the scale of the devastation was now starting to become clear.

'It's round the back,' the fire officer said, beckoning them to follow him. 'We've not moved him. Fortunately the fire never properly reached the back of the house, so we were able to leave him in situ.'

'And it was the fall that did it?' Wendy asked.

'You tell me. Not my area of expertise I'm afraid, but it certainly didn't do him any good judging by the mess he made. Looks to me as if he was trying to jump into the pool. There's a pair of french windows on one of the upper floors that were open. Some of the other windows had blown out, but those look like they were physically opened. Again, it's not my place to say, but if you ask me I reckon that's where he jumped from. It's two floors up, so missing and hitting the concrete would probably have done the job.'

Wendy shook her head as she imagined the scene. Would she rather burn to death in a fire or die from trying — and failing — to escape it?

The back of the house was even more impressive than the front, being set within sprawling grounds that couldn't realistically be called a garden. The pool was huge, and the water rippled gently in the rising light, as if oblivious to what had happened here only recently.

'Bloody hell, you don't hang about do you?' Culverhouse called over to Dr Janet Grey, the pathologist, who was talking to a fully white-suited forensics officer outside the huge white tent that had been erected over the body.

'Always preferable to having your trained chimps trampling all over my evidence, Detective Chief Inspector. And good morning to you too.'

The friendly banter between Culverhouse and Grey had been going on for a number of years. Culverhouse occasionally fancied that he could see himself getting on well with a woman like Grey outside of work, but it wasn't a possibility he ever seriously entertained.

'*Our* evidence, Dr Grey. You'll have to learn to share. What've we got?'

'You already know what we've got, which is why you're here. Deceased male in his late sixties — identity known to you, I believe — death appears to have been caused by multiple heavy trauma. Probably from jumping out of there,' she said, pointing to the second-floor balcony. 'I'm sure the post mortem will find smoke in his lungs, but that's to be expected.'

'Any chance he didn't jump voluntarily?' Culverhouse asked.

'Well, if he didn't his assailant will be a shoe-in for the hammer throw at the Olympics. He's cleared a fair lateral distance for someone who just fell. Or was pushed. But either way I don't suppose it matters. If he was jumping because of the fire and the fire was caused by arson, someone else is responsible for his death either way. It'll be another black mark on his rap sheet when you catch him.'

'Or her.'

'Oh no,' the pathologist replied, smiling sweetly at Culverhouse. 'Ladies would never do such a thing. We're all tucked up in bed at that time of night after a long day cleaning and ironing, aren't we Detective Sergeant Knight?'

'Perhaps I might be tempted. If I owned an iron,' Wendy joked.

'Any other signs of anything?' Culverhouse asked, ignoring their jibes.

'Bit early to say just yet, but I can't see any other signs of trauma. I think we can probably rule out a fight or any sort of altercation. His eyes were open when he hit the deck so he was probably conscious at the time. Again, we'll be able to confirm all that during the post mortem, as well as checking for any sort of chemical foul play. Why, what other signs are you looking for?'

Jack exchanged a glance with Wendy before he spoke. 'Well, let's just say I don't think anything would surprise me. The bloke you've got in there,' he said, jabbing a finger towards the tent, 'didn't exactly spend his life making friends. I can imagine one or two people might've wanted to make sure he'd gone to meet his maker — whichever sort of sick bastard would want to make someone like him.'

'Arson would be a bit risky, though, wouldn't it?' Dr Grey said. 'I mean, if you want someone dead there are much better ways. Especially considering the time of night the fire happened, and the fact it was started at the front door, quite a long way away from the bedroom he jumped out of. Seems like sheer luck that he missed the pool and died.'

'Maybe they weren't trying to kill him,' Wendy offered. 'Maybe they just wanted to burn his house down and cause him some damage. A warning, perhaps.'

'Some fucking warning,' Culverhouse remarked, looking up at the charred remains of the once-impressive building.

'Yeah, well, maybe things just got out of hand. Can't always predict what fire's going to do.'

'Either way, it's irrelevant at the moment. What we do know is that someone deliberately set fire to this house and that Freddie Galloway died as a result. We're looking at aggravated arson and manslaughter. Minimum.'

'Do you want to see the body?' Janet Grey asked.

'No thanks. Not had my breakfast yet. Email me the photos later. Should perk my afternoon right up.'

10

'That's it, my son! Left hook, quick in with an uppercut on the right – yes! Come on, feel that burn!'

Tyrone Golds grunted as the beads of sweat cascaded over his eyebrows and splashed gently to the floor, the salty sting getting in his eyes as he felt the lactic acid build up in his arms. It was a feeling he loved – something that made him feel free and liberated. He'd been boxing since he was six, and he adored every second of it.

A couple of hours with the punchbag in his local boxing club was his idea of a morning well spent. And having someone like Kai here to spot him and spur him on was an added bonus. Friends and trainers had always said he could have performed competitively – perhaps even professionally – but that had never interested him. He liked the spit-and-sawdust backstreet boxing clubs like this one. He liked being his own man. If he was completely honest with himself, he didn't have that competitive edge that he'd need in order to win. He just loved boxing, loved feeling the burn, loved pummelling the shit out of dangling bags.

Sure, his technique was impressive. It would be if you'd spent as many years as he had, boxing almost every single day without fail. But he'd had no desire to compete or get involved with boxing on any professional level. After all, he knew far too many people who'd combined their loves with their jobs and had ultimately become disappointed. As soon as you start receiving money for something you love doing, it becomes a burden. And he never wanted boxing to become a burden. He never wanted to fall out of love with it.

After all, it had kept him out of trouble — largely. There'd been the odd occasions where he'd been tempted across the line, but that was completely unavoidable. Growing up on the estate he'd lived on as a child, he could no more have avoided criminality than he could breathing oxygen. It was there, all around him. For many of his peers, it was a way of life. It was about survival. And Tyrone'd had plenty of surviving to do.

After his dad had walked out on him, his mother and his older sister Shanice, things had changed almost overnight. His mum had to go from being the stay-at-home mother to the working mother, grinding her fingers to the bone on twelve-hour shifts, leaving Shanice to bring up both Tyrone and herself. His mother never really recovered from the heartbreak, and Tyrone credited that alongside long hours working in a pharmaceuticals factory for the cancer that caused her early death at the age of thirty-five.

It was barely a week after Shanice's sixteenth birthday, which at least meant they weren't taken into care but were instead allowed to take on the council flat as tenants in their own right. Boxing had been his way of channelling his anger and frustration, and he credited it with saving him on more than one occasion.

Life on the estate hadn't been easy. It wasn't exactly a cakewalk for anyone, but a recently bereaved sixteen-year-old is never going to be able to give you the best upbringing. It wasn't through lack of effort or dedication, by any means. Although Shanice had shown great academic promise and was planning to go on to do A levels, she'd left school that summer and gone straight into work, choosing instead to provide for herself and her brother. That was something that had made Tyrone feel both grateful and guilty.

'Bruv, I'm done,' he said, dropping into a crouched position as he felt the burn in his biceps and triceps.

'You getting old!' Kai quipped as he slapped Tyrone on the back playfully and helped him back to his feet.

'Three rounds, bruv. Three rounds. You and me. I'm tellin' you, I wouldn't even need the last two.'

The pair laughed and joked as they made their way towards the showers. The banter and camaraderie was one of the upsides of coming here, as far as Tyrone was concerned. There had, at times, been a similar sort of brotherhood and solidarity on the estate, but there was always that sinister edge — the chance that things could very quickly turn nasty. And they often did. He'd seen friends shot and killed in gang attacks, flats torched by rival groups.

But at the boxing club, things never threatened to turn violent – despite the fact that they were all here specifically to fight. Boxing, though, was different. There was no malice involved. It was pure sport.

He'd known fairly quickly how boxing had changed him, had made him see things in a different light. That was why he'd decided to earn some money by training others on the estate to box. He didn't have as much of the anger, didn't feel the need to rail back against the system that had treated him so badly. He knew a number of boys on the estate who could benefit from that, but precious few had ever shown a serious interest. Once they were stuck in their ruts, they were happy to stay there, chasing the next batch of notes, constantly looking over their shoulders for guns or knives.

He'd earned the nickname Bruno for a while – a nod to the success of British boxer Frank Bruno at the time. But that was a nickname he'd left behind. Too many people associated it with one or two of the times he'd been tempted the wrong way, had succumbed to the offer of a quick buck in exchange for bending the law ever so slightly. After the last time, he decided he was going back to being good old Tyrone Golds. A man with a proper name and nothing to hide.

But deep down he knew that was just another cover in itself. Because, where he came from, everyone had something to hide.

11

By the time Jack and Wendy were back in the office, Steve Wing had already pulled out all the information he could find on Freddie Galloway's history with the police. Culverhouse knew most of it, but he still listened intently as Steve updated the team on what he had.

'There's no immediate family or next of kin that we know about. His parents are long gone, and he was an only child.'

'What about a wife or girlfriend?' Wendy asked.

Steve shuffled awkwardly as Culverhouse let out a small laugh before speaking. 'Let's just say he was a confirmed bachelor.'

'He was gay?'

'You'd be a braver person than me to want to tell him that. Freddie Galloway was old school. He did things his own way. He never married or had a girlfriend that anyone knew about. You'd be surprised how many of those old-time gangsters had their own special... predilictions.'

Steve cleared his throat and began talking again. 'Basically, he was a career criminal who somehow always managed to squirm out of our hands. He's been arrested, questioned, even charged on one occasion for harassment and intimidation of a witness, but it was thrown out of court when the victim decided to retract their claim. Because he was being intimidated, I presume. He's got a rap sheet as long as my arm. All of it either unproven, or not followed up because of retracted statements or lost evidence. Looks as if he knew how to play the system perfectly.'

'Yet the silly fucker couldn't outwit some bloke with a jerry can,' Culverhouse quipped.

'I imagine he will have made a lot of enemies. Particularly after the Trenton-Lowe job.'

The three older male officers shared a knowing look, having all been serving police officers at the time of the robbery, before Culverhouse explained for the benefit of Wendy, Debbie and Ryan.

'Trenton-Lowe was a roofing supplier about thirty miles away. Mainly tiles. This was probably a good ten or so years ago now.'

'Eleven,' Frank corrected. 'I'd just had my gallstone op.'

'Lovely. Cheers, Frank. Good to know we can all set our clocks by your failing body. So, eleven years ago, they were starting to build the new pikey camp on the outskirts of town.'

'Do you mean travellers' site, Detective Chief Inspector?' Ryan asked.

Culverhouse stared at her for a moment. 'Whatever you bloody well want to call it, eleven years ago they were starting to build it, alright? Any more interruptions?' The team remained silent. 'Right. Now, they're all permanent brick structures up there, so they needed a lot of roofing materials. These guys do everything in cash, and the bloke who ran Trenton-Lowe did them a deal for a massive number of roof tiles and other stuff. We're talking about tiles, membranes and gear for nearly a hundred buildings. Almost half a million quid. In cash.

'Now, the bloke who owned Trenton-Lowe wasn't going to say no to that, and he was greedy enough that he didn't fancy accounting for all the tax on it either. So he stuck it in a safe for the time being and hired a security guard to watch the premises overnight. Somehow, word gets to Freddie Galloway that this cash is sitting there in this safe. Whether it was an employee at the warehouse or what, we don't know. But one night Freddie and his chums waltzed in, coshed the security guard and went for the safe. But someone tipped off the local police. Before they could get anything they'd scarpered, but not before one of Freddie's men shot a police officer in the head. Somehow he survived, but never worked again.'

'Jesus Christ. And he wasn't sent down for this?' Ryan asked.

'Nope. Slippery as an eel. Couldn't prove he was involved, even though word on the street is he was in there with them. The guy who pulled the trigger, John Lucas, was caught. The officer he shot recognised him. Lucas must've thought he'd killed him and got rid of the witness, but he survived. When he was arrested, he blabbed everything he knew, which wasn't much. He claimed Freddie Galloway was the brains behind the operation. Shortly after they arrested Galloway, Lucas retracted his statement. Mentioned something about not wanting his mum to get hurt. He wouldn't say any more than that. General consensus is that Galloway made some sort of threat towards Lucas's family, causing him to retract what he'd said.'

'Wow. Sounds like a nice guy.'

'Yeah, he probably wasn't the only one who wanted him dead, either. See, the story from John Lucas and Benjamin Newell — the two blokes who went down for it — was that the safe was never opened. They both told identical stories. But when the Trenton-Lowe bosses opened the safe with the police there, the money was gone.'

'So who took it?' Ryan asked.

'No idea. No-one knows. Theory is it was either taken by Galloway after the others escaped and before the police turned up, or that it wasn't even in the safe and had been emptied out by Galloway's inside man before the robbery even took place.'

'Christ. I'm starting to see why someone would want to pop him off myself.'

'I was there that day in court. Lots of officers were, even though it wasn't our patch. When a fellow officer takes a bullet in the line of duty, you feel obliged to stand together.' Culverhouse paused for a moment. The rest of the team knew he was also referring to the death of Luke Baxter, an officer on their team who'd been killed two years earlier. 'Lucas seemed angry more than anything. Not at the police, but at Galloway. Even though he'd retracted his statement, you could still see it in him. He despised Galloway. When the judge asked him if he had any last words Lucas wanted him to take into account, he said "I hope Freddie Galloway rots in hell". The judge asked him what he meant and he stayed silent. Eighteen years, I think his sentence was. Word from those on his side of the fence is that when he was inside he made all sorts of comments about getting vengeance for what Galloway did to him.'

Wendy raised her hand as she stared at her computer screen.

'Erm, this John Lucas. How old would you say he is now?'

'Dunno. Must be in his fifties. Why?' Culverhouse asked.

'Does he look like this?' Wendy showed him the picture on her computer screen, which she'd found on the Police National Computer.

'Yeah. That's the bastard. Recognise him anywhere.'

'In that case, we might have a lead. John Lucas was released from Belmarsh yesterday morning.'

12

While the others were left trying to find out John Lucas's parole address, Culverhouse went back into his office. Wendy followed him, keen to catch him as quickly as possible before things really kicked off.

'I know this is a bad time,' she said, closing the door behind her, 'but I need to get it sorted before this case starts to take over.'

'What is it?' Culverhouse barked, putting a pile of papers down on his desk with more force than was necessary.

'My inspectors' exams. The next opening is coming up in a few weeks and I think I'd like to go for it this year. Problem is, the first exam is on a date I'm scheduled on shift.'

'A few weeks? You'd need longer than that to revise, surely?' Culverhouse asked, narrowing his eyes at her.

'I reckon I could cram. It's either that or wait another

year for the exams to come round again. I might as well go for it.'

Culverhouse thought for a moment before shaking his head. 'No. The only way you're going to manage that is if you sit at home reading Blackstone's back to back, over and over. I can't have your head stuck in that mode while I need you active on the team. There's a good chance you'll have to do overtime, too.'

This wasn't the response Wendy had expected. She thought he might make some sort of derogatory comment – she'd have been amazed if he didn't – but the suggestion that Wendy should take her inspectors' exams had been his, and she wasn't going to let him forget that.

'But I reckon I could do it. Most of the stuff I've been revising is stuff I've already got a decent grasp of. And yeah, there's a good chance I might not pass, but if that's the case then I'll still have to wait until next year anyway. What's the harm in trying this year too, even if I fail spectacularly?'

'Like I said. I need you on the ball, not thinking about exams and revision. Go for it next year instead. Then you've got a year and a bit to revise and get yourself ready. That way, the team doesn't lose out.' Culverhouse sat down in his chair and made a charade of looking something up on his computer, even though Wendy knew damn well he was just trying to get her to shut up and leave.

She tried not to rise to the bait. 'The team won't lose out. If anything, it'll gain from my experience and new rank. It'll take some of the pressure off you, too. It was your idea.'

Culverhouse steepled his hands and took a deep breath. 'I'm aware of that, Knight. And I've got absolutely nothing against you going for the inspectors' exams, but all I'm saying is that now's not the time. Since I mentioned it all that time ago, you've said nothing about it. I thought you'd ignored it, weren't interested. And now months later you come in and tell me you want to take time off in a couple of weeks' time for it? On the morning a new major investigation kicks off? You're one for bloody timing, I'll give you that.'

'I've not done it on purpose,' Wendy said, feeling somewhat affronted at the attitude Culverhouse had taken. 'I've been thinking about it for a while, ever since you mentioned it.'

'But you didn't think to tell me? Perhaps warn me that you were going to be going for it?'

'It was your idea!' Wendy said, raising her voice. She knew he was being completely unreasonable, but at the same time he had a knack of making his argument sound perfectly fair.

'Look, we're just going round in circles here,' Culverhouse said, standing and walking over to the office door. 'I've said no, and that's that. Alright?'

He opened the door and looked at Wendy, who walked out of the office and back into the incident room without looking at him once.

13

It felt so good to be free, John Lucas thought, as he poured himself a cup of tea. It was these little luxuries that he would come to appreciate in the outside world: making a cup of tea whenever he wanted one, perhaps adding a chocolate biscuit or two, looking out across the town.

He wouldn't stay here for long. The house held too many memories for him. It had been his family home once, but after the death of his mother while he was inside, the place didn't hold the same charm anymore. It held memories – plenty of those. And whilst it had been kept clean and tidy thanks to his mother's regular cleaner staying on after she'd died – paid for through provision in her will – it was definitely dated.

He'd need to do a lot of work to get rid of the detailed flowery wallpaper and wood-chip ceilings. The bathroom and kitchen could do with being ripped out and totally redone too, but there wasn't much point. The money left in his mother's will would barely cover a few carpets. He thanked his lucky stars his release date had come up before the money had run out for the cleaner, else the whole place would be suitable only for demolition.

Valentina was a good worker, it seemed. She'd definitely done a good job of keeping the house neat and tidy. It was a shame she wasn't a painter and decorator, too.

Nonetheless, selling this place should bring him in a few quid, he thought. He hadn't been keeping up to date with house prices recently, but he reckoned it'd probably fetch just shy of three hundred grand, which would all be his seeing as his mum had paid the mortgage off years ago.

Maybe he'd get an estate agent round later in the week. He had enough to be worrying about in the meantime. He'd get them to handle it, put it up for sale, get him a buyer. He could use some of the cash to buy himself a flat or a small house and keep the rest as a buffer while he tried to move on with his life. He could certainly do with a job — he'd have overheads that the cash buffer wouldn't maintain. He wouldn't need much, but it had to be something he'd enjoy. The probation service had paired him up with a shoe repairs company who often took on ex-offenders, but he wasn't sure if he'd be happy there long-term. And his happiness had to come first. After everything that had happened, he was going to spend his time looking after number one.

He'd learnt a lot on the inside. That's the sort of thing that happens when you're given time to think. Especially when you're given eleven years to think. By the end of it all he'd just wanted to get out, wanted to make a fresh start and try again. He'd still be under the watchful eye of the authorities — he'd have a probation officer visiting him regularly — but to all intents and purposes he was a free man. Certainly freer than he'd been a day or two earlier, anyway.

He'd done what he'd needed to do to come to terms with everything that had happened. Forgive and forget, they all said. That had never seemed possible. But sometimes — just sometimes — something would happen that'd mean it all became irrelevant. Events had a funny way of putting things in perspective. And now he was able to move on with his life, free from the bitterness and anger that had consumed him for so many years.

True enough, the decision had been his. It had been a spur of the moment thing. He didn't feel he'd been left with any option. It was the only way out. At least, it had seemed that way at the time. Soon enough, the testosterone and adrenaline had died down and he'd been able to see that it was a bad move. But still, he couldn't shake the feeling that his hand had been forced, that he didn't have another option. And when all was said and done, that decision had been forced upon him by Freddie bloody Galloway, whether he liked it or not.

He started to feel the anger rising again, then told himself that he didn't need to feel angry any more. This was all over. He was able to move on now, to become a bigger and better person. He couldn't let what happened all those years ago rule his life any more. If he did, it threatened to consume him and take over. Now he was able to make a clean break. Now his destiny was in his own hands.

He sipped at the hot mug of tea, not minding the fact that it was scalding his lips. To be able to have a piping hot cup of tea was a luxury compared to the lukewarm shit he'd been given in prison. What he did mind, though, was that his doorbell had just rung, quickly followed by a knock at the door.

His probation officer wasn't due to visit until tomorrow. What concerned him the most was that many of the old gang still knew where he lived. He'd never been afraid of that, never worried about hiding it. There was honour amongst thieves, as the saying went, and at the end of the day no-one had any reason to hold a grudge against him. But spending his life mixed up with bad people had made him unavoidably paranoid.

He went to the curtains in the living room and peered out through the gap, looking at the two figures standing by his front door. In that instant, he knew this wasn't going to be good.

14

Tyrone grunted and let out a groan of intense pleasure tinged with an undercurrent of pain. The pain wasn't a bad thing, though; it felt good. It was all part of it, as far as he was concerned.

He felt the strong release as he ejaculated onto the bedsheets below him, feeling the movement slow and stop as Lenny's hand returned to Tyrone's right hip, before Lenny eased himself out, allowing Tyrone to flop down onto the bed, avoiding the sticky patch he'd just created.

He'd been coming to see Lenny for almost two years now, and he felt they'd built up a connection, a bond. He knew damn well there was no way he'd build up a real relationship with a rent boy, a male prostitute whose job was to make men feel special, but after the number of times he'd been to see Lenny, Lenny had got to know exactly what Tyrone had liked. It had got better every time.

Immediately afterwards came the guilt. Every single

time. It flooded him with the undeniable feeling that what he had done was wrong, that if anyone he knew found out about it his life would be over. He asked himself the same old questions: Why did he come here? Why couldn't he have satisfied those urges on his own? But that was nothing compared to the absolute pleasure he'd felt in the preceding minutes, which was the whole reason he'd kept coming here, time after time, for the past couple of years.

He'd be crucified if anyone he knew found out. In the circles he moved in, homosexuality was worse than a sin. Not that Tyrone was gay, of course — he'd never use that word to describe himself. He just had certain ... urges. He'd never enter into a relationship with a man. There was no way he could even if he wanted to, but the thought often made him feel repulsed. He knew he'd been conditioned to feel that way due to his upbringing and cultural background, but that knowledge changed nothing. It was built into his DNA to feel that what he was doing was wrong. Worse than wrong.

'You know, you lads need to give yourselves a break,' Lenny said, as he pulled on his jeans.

'How d'you mean?' Tyrone replied, refusing to meet his eye.

'You black guys. You always pretend like it hasn't happened, like it's not perfectly normal and natural to have desires.'

Tyrone sat on the edge of the bed, ignoring the pain from his backside, and leant down to pick up his boxer shorts before putting them on.

'Dunno what you're talking about. I'm just tired. Had a long week.'

'You've been having long weeks for the past two years then. All your lot have. You all act the same afterwards. Like it's some big sin. That mama's going to disown you for it if she finds out.'

Tyrone instinctively closed the space between him and Lenny, keen to intimidate him but at the same time not wanting to get too close right now. 'You know nothing about my mum, alright? And you can cut out the racism 'n'all.'

Lenny looked at Tyrone and shook his head as he watched him put his own jeans on before pulling a tight t-shirt over his muscled torso. 'It's not racism, sweetie. It's a pattern I've noticed. You all seem to do it. Why can't you just let go and enjoy yourselves?'

Tyrone fished a wad of notes out of his pocket and threw two twenties and a ten onto the bed. 'Fifty quid, isn't it?' he asked, knowing damn well the special price they'd agreed months ago.

'Only for you. Seriously, though. You need to let loose. It's not good for you to ignore it and carry this round like it's some sort of burden. Black guys can be gay, you know. You're not exempt.'

Tyrone stopped tying his lace for a moment and closed his eyes, trying to calm himself and avoid getting worked up. 'Like I said. I'm just tired. It's been a long week.'

Lenny was less than convinced, but he could see he wasn't going to get any further with this. 'Alright. I won't push. But just know that it's never as bad as you think, alright? The world's moved on. The vast majority of people are cool with it. You might be surprised.'

Tyrone nodded and picked up his gym bag before going to walk past Lenny and head for the door. As he did, Lenny took hold of his arm.

'Same time next week?'

Tyrone avoided Lenny's eye and pulled free from his grip. 'I'll let you know.'

15

'John Lucas?' Culverhouse said as the man in front of him opened the door.

'Yeah, why?'

'Can we come in?' the DCI replied, already pushing his way past John Lucas and into the house, Wendy following behind him.

'Doesn't look like I've got much choice, does it?'

'Just wondered if we could ask you a few questions, that's all,' Culverhouse called from the living room. 'Nice wallpaper, by the way.'

'It's my mum's. Was. And anyway, I deal with the probation service now. You lot had your moment eleven years ago. I'm clean now.'

Culverhouse snorted as he put the photo of John's mum and dad back on the mantelpiece. 'Once a con, always a con.'

John stood in the doorway and folded his arms. 'I know

what this is all about. This is because of that copper, isn't it? You lot never could admit that people make mistakes, they change. It was eleven years ago. It was a mistake.'

Culverhouse walked slowly over to John until he was almost nose-to-nose with him. '"That copper" had a name. His name was Owen McCready. He was a dedicated, loyal police officer who worked to keep the public safe. He had a bullet lodged in his pre-frontal cortex. A bullet fired from your gun. He spent four months in hospital, came out a changed man who managed to ruin his marriage and never worked again. He had a name.'

John nodded, holding Culverhouse's eye contact. 'Like I said. It was a mistake. I served my time.'

'You didn't serve a quarter of what you deserved,' Culverhouse said, sitting down in an armchair. 'Now. Where were you last night?'

'I was here,' Lucas replied. 'I'm not allowed anywhere else.'

'I know you're not. You tagged?'

'No.'

'So how are we meant to know where you were last night?' Culverhouse asked.

Wendy hovered behind John Lucas, keen to see how this was going to play out.

'Listen, I was released on parole because I'd served my time and the prison reported to the parole board that I'd been on my best behaviour. Read the judgement. It declared me to be a reformed character who deserved a second chance. What do you reckon the odds are of me breaking the terms of my probation on the first bloody night I'm released? I was here. All night. And I'm still here.'

'Do you live alone?'

'Yes. My mum died while I was inside.'

'Hence the wallpaper,' Culverhouse quipped, gesturing at the walls. Lucas ignored him. 'I presume the name Freddie Galloway means something to you?'

John Lucas laughed. 'You know damn well it does. You've not come here knocking on random doors, have you? You know about me, and you know about Freddie Galloway.'

'And what do you know about him? Any idea what he's up to at the moment?'

Lucas swallowed hard. 'I don't know and I don't care. I've put that all behind me now.'

Culverhouse nodded as he looked at him. 'And what if I was to tell you that he's currently lying on a slab in the mortuary, having been moved there from a slab in his back garden?'

He watched as Lucas registered what he was telling him, but he couldn't see any signs of recognition or reaction to what he'd said.

'I don't know,' Lucas said, eventually. 'I want to say "good", but I don't see how that would help anyone.'

Wendy gave Culverhouse a look that said he should just arrest Lucas and get it over with. PACE guidelines suggested that arrests should be made immediately, meaning that anything the suspect said could be taken down as evidence to be used against him. All the time

Culverhouse spent talking to Lucas before arresting him was potentially wasted, and anything he said could easily be thrown out in court. But Culverhouse had his own way of doing things and tended to follow his nose rather than the guidelines – something which had rarely let him down in the past.

'What were you wearing last night?' Culverhouse asked.

'Uh, a t-shirt and jeans I think. Why?'

'Where are they?'

'In my washing basket, upstairs in the bedroom.'

Culverhouse nodded to Wendy to go upstairs and retrieve the washing basket as evidence. Potentially, they could find traces of accelerant on the material or other evidence which would link John Lucas to the scene of the arson attack on Freddie Galloway's house.

'Righto. In the meantime, Mr Lucas. You're coming with me.' Culverhouse read him his rights as dictated by the Police and Criminal Evidence Act, put the handcuffs on him and led him out to the car.

16

By the time Jack and Wendy had got back from John Lucas's house, the team had begun gathering together all the information they had relating to the man and his past. Having had Lucas booked into the custody suite, they'd left him to sit in a cell while they gathered everything they needed for the interview.

They knew they'd have twenty-four hours in which to speak to him and gather enough evidence to convince the Crown Prosecution Service to authorise charging Lucas. If that time passed, they'd either need to request an extension – something which was far from guaranteed – or release him.

'There's quite a lot of information on the armed robbery case itself, and even more on things John Lucas said afterwards, while he was in prison,' DC Ryan Mackenzie said. 'Two men were convicted over the Trenton-Lowe robbery. One of them was John Lucas. He blabbed more or less straight away about who else was involved. He named Galloway, but later retracted that. Afterwards, he'd only ever give the nicknames. The officers who questioned him at the time suspected he knew their real names, but didn't want to say.'

'Why would he do that, though? I mean, if he was blabbing anyway, why not go the whole hog?' Wendy asked.

'To make us think he's told us everything,' Culverhouse said. 'Seem like you're being helpful and cooperative, but hold a load back. Tried and tested.'

Ryan continued. 'The names he gave were Footloose, Peter and Bruno. Now, the officers at the time assumed Footloose was Freddie Galloway, otherwise known as Footloose Freddie. That was no surprise to anyone. They later found out that Peter was actually a man by the name of Benjamin Newell.'

'Why Peter?' Steve asked.

'Comes from "Peterman", a slang term for a safecracker. He was the one who was meant to break into the safe and steal the cash. But something went wrong. In interview he said he was told the safe was a completely different type. Said the information was duff. He wouldn't blame it on anyone in particular, though. Again, the general consensus was Freddie Galloway.'

'Another motive for murder,' Culverhouse interrupted. 'If you're due a huge wad of cash and some dozy bastard fucks it up by giving you dodgy info, you'd want to do something about it, wouldn't you? Might be worth looking at

Newell's finances and recent history. See if there's something that might've urged him to act now.'

'Well that's the thing,' Ryan said. 'Why wait that long? Newell was only in prison for three and a half years. He could've done Galloway over any time he wanted. Why wait until now?'

'Because doing it the day he got out of prison would've looked a bit too obvious, don't you think? Look how quickly we descended on John Lucas when we realised he'd been released the same day Freddie Galloway's place burnt to the ground. That's why I'm not convinced it was him.'

'What if it was Newell, and he'd done it that day because he knew it'd frame Lucas?' Steve offered.

'Possible,' Culverhouse replied.

'Thing is,' Ryan continued, 'There are a number of statements from prison officers and other people Lucas had spoken to. He regularly and openly spoke about how Galloway had "done him over" and left him to face the music alone. Galloway – assuming he's Footloose – and this Bruno guy left via the back entrance and managed to escape. Lucas and Newell – Headache and Peter – went back out the front.'

'Headache?' Culverhouse asked, his face contorted.

Ryan shrugged and shook her head slightly. 'No idea. Never got to the bottom of that one. But they were stopped by a patrol officer who heard the call over the radio. He was in the area at the time. He recognised Lucas, and made the stupid mistake of telling him so. He took a bullet to the head. When he came round in hospital he gave Lucas's name and they matched gunshot residue found on his clothing. Seems he'd been so confident he'd killed the officer, he didn't even bother to chuck his clothes in the wash. Newell was driving the getaway van. He drove off after Lucas shot the police officer, and was stopped less than half a mile down the road. He drove into the side of a chip shop trying to escape from traffic officers who tried to pull him over for having no insurance.'

Culverhouse guffawed. 'You couldn't make it up. What a bunch of twats.'

'Lucas was the one who seemed to suffer most. He got the longest sentence, obviously, for pulling the trigger. Apparently he was more than willing to give up all sorts of information by the time he was up for parole. Possible he was trying to buy his way out, but the parole board said he seemed genuinely remorseful and that he wanted to help.'

Culverhouse snorted. 'Yeah, we've seen that before. It's amazing how many born-again-Christians pop up six weeks before their parole hearings. John Lucas might've been able to pull the wool over the parole board's eyes, but I'm something different altogether.'

'You can say that again,' Frank Vine muttered under his breath.

Culverhouse, although blessed with supersonic hearing, pretended not to hear him.

'Right. Well, I think we'd better go and have a word or two with Mr Lucas, don't you?'

17

Benjamin Newell beamed with pride as he watched his new wife strutting her stuff on the dance floor, surrounded by friends and family. The day had gone beautifully, and everyone seemed to have a great time. Lisa had used the bride's prerogative to make him wait an extra ten minutes, turning up to the ceremony fashionably late. But he hadn't doubted that she'd come – not really. He'd never been able to rely on anyone up until meeting Lisa, but he knew he could trust her fully. It was the first time he'd ever been able to give himself to anyone completely, and it felt hugely refreshing.

He sidled up to the bar and ordered another pint of Foster's. It was easy drinking, and today had been a warm day – not to mention the heat building up inside the venue now that the disco lights were on and the guests were busy dancing away. Some'd had more to drink than others, as was customary at British weddings, and the guy standing to his left seemed to be swaying rhythmically to a completely different song than the one that was actually playing.

Benjamin eyed him, trying to figure out who he was. After the ceremony itself, dozens of people had turned up to the evening party – many of them friends or acquaintances of Lisa, people he didn't know. He smiled at the man, hoping to strike up conversation.

'Having a good time?' he asked him, watching as the man turned his head in the direction of the words.

'Yeah, great!' the man said, lifting his pint glass up in salute. Benjamin watched as the frothy head slopped up the inside of the glass and over the man's hand, falling to the wooden floor with a gentle splat.

'So you a friend of Lisa's, then?' he asked, struggling to make himself heard over the sound of a new song that'd just begun playing.

'One word for it, yeah. We work together at Sanderson Lees.'

Benjamin nodded as he tried to secretly guess what subject the man taught. He had the physique of a PE teacher, but he drank like a janitor. Maybe an English teacher who looked after himself, or a groundsman. So many people worked at the Sanderson Lees Academy, he wouldn't be surprised if they had engineers and accountants on the payroll.

'What do you teach?' Benjamin asked him, stepping closer to avoid having to shout over the music.

'Business Studies,' the man replied. 'I trained as a PE

teacher and ended up covering other stuff. Always the way in this job. Never end up doing what you planned to do.'

Benjamin nodded, convinced he'd heard Lisa say something similar at some point. 'So have you been working there long?'

'Fucking long enough,' the man replied. 'Sorry, I'm Ollie. Mr Hardcastle to my students,' he added, guffawing as if this were the funniest joke he'd ever told. Benjamin presumed it probably was.

'Nice to meet you,' he replied.

'You know, me and Lisa had a bit of a thing a few years back. When she started working there. Didn't last long, mind.'

Benjamin swallowed hard, forcing back the urge to feel angry. He had no right to feel angry – this was his wedding day, and Lisa was now his wife. Why should he care who she'd dated before he'd even met her? It had nothing to do with how things were now. But he still couldn't shake the instinctive reaction that was pure anger.

'Really,' he said, not as a question, before taking a large gulp of his lager.

'Oh yes,' the man slurred. 'Then again, that's what happens when you start at a new place, isn't it? Got to test the water. See what's on offer. Do a few test drives.'

Benjamin gritted his teeth as Ollie raised his pint glass in salute again, grinning from ear to ear like a Cheshire cat.

'I tell you,' he continued, leaning in close enough for Benjamin to smell the beer fumes on his breath, 'I still remember every minute of it. You've got a good one there, buddy. Arse like a hot potato. And the way she does that thing where she wraps her legs around you and—'

Ollie gurgled as Benjamin's hand wrapped around his windpipe, squeezing tightly, lifting him up onto his tiptoes. His back was against the wooden pillar, and he could see the venom in Benjamin's eyes.

'Alright! Alright!' he squealed as Benjamin's best man, Cameron, took him by the arm and defused the situation before too many people had noticed.

Benjamin looked around and saw Lisa on the dance floor with her friends, completely oblivious to what had happened. In that moment, he realised he'd got away with it.

'I think it'd be a good idea if you fucked off, don't you?' Cameron told Ollie. 'I don't know who you are, and I don't care. But this is his wedding day and we're not having any of that shit here, alright?'

'But he attacked me!' Ollie slurred, reaching for his pint on the bar.

'You've had enough of that, mate,' Cameron said, taking the glass from him. 'And if I know my mate, he doesn't do things like that without a good reason. Which means you've been an arsehole. Which means you're leaving.'

Cameron was, by now, almost toe-to-toe with Ollie, who took the hint and slunk off towards the exit.

'What was that all about?' Cameron asked, once Ollie had gone.

'Nothing. Just some dickhead making comments about Lisa. Forget it.'

Cameron nodded, knowing there must be more to it than that. 'Pop outside for a smoke?' he asked, pulling a packet of cigarettes out of his pocket. Benjamin hadn't smoked for years, other than the odd occasion when he'd had too much to drink. Right now, though, the thought was very appealing. He craved the taste of a cigarette, the calming nicotine.

The pair stepped outside and enjoying the calm breeze that cooled them down slightly after the heat of the bar. Benjamin had barely taken two drags on his cigarette when he heard the familiar voice of Ollie, accompanied by the sound of unsteady footsteps crunching their way across the gravel.

'Think you're the fucking hard man, do you? Cat that got the cream.'

'Fuck off, mate. We told you to go,' Cameron called, before turning to Benjamin. 'I'll go in and get a couple of the lads. Just in case.'

'Yeah, go on! Run off back inside!' Ollie yelled. 'And what about you, mister married man? I bet you're proud, ain't you? Proud to get my sloppy seconds. Hell, she's everyone's sloppy seconds, the filthy little slag.'

Before he knew what he was doing, Benjamin sprinted across the gravel and launched himself at Ollie, pinning him to the ground as he pummelled his fists into the man's face, before pushing his forearm against Ollie's windpipe, lifting his knee and ramming it into his groin, over and over.

'Think you're the fucking smart man, do you?'

Benjamin yelled, the rage and fury washing over him in a way it hadn't done for years.

He didn't know how long he'd been there, but he was dragged back into reality by the force of a couple of his friends pulling him off of Ollie and standing him up a few feet away.

Benjamin ran his finger through his hair and inspected his bloodied knuckles, before turning to head back towards the bar. As he did so, he could see Lisa standing not ten feet away from him, tears staining her cheeks.

18

Jack and Wendy walked into the interview room and sat down, John Lucas having already been seated across the table next to his solicitor, a chubby man by the name of Matthew Chamberlain, who looked as if he'd been dragged out of the pub to be here.

Wendy was the first to speak. 'Okay, John. We want to speak to you with regards to an event that took place last night in the village of Little Walgrave. Have you ever been there?'

Lucas looked at his solicitor, who nodded to indicate that he should talk. 'I've probably passed through a few times, in the car. It's not far away from here.'

'And do you know anyone who lives there?'

Lucas was silent for a few moments. 'Depends what you mean by that.'

'Tell us what you mean by it,' Wendy said.

'Freddie Galloway lives there. Lived there,' he corrected himself. 'But I wasn't exactly best mates with him, so if you mean was there anyone there who I'd go and visit, the answer's no.'

'We're not talking about visits, though, are we?' Culverhouse interrupted. 'We're talking about a case of arson. So, tell us more about why you weren't exactly best mates with Freddie Galloway.'

Lucas looked down at his lap and let out a noise that sounded like it came from somewhere between a laugh and a snort of disbelief. 'You already know all this. I was caught and sent down. I've done my time.'

'With respect, that doesn't tell us anything,' Wendy said. 'Was there bad blood between you and Freddie Galloway?'

Chamberlain leaned over and whispered something in his client's ear.

Lucas looked up at Wendy. 'Look, everyone knows I didn't like him. But I didn't do anything to him. I've changed, alright? You can ask anyone. I wouldn't have been paroled if they thought I was a danger to anyone, so why would I go and burn a bloke's house down hours later? I've learned to forgive and forget.'

'Tell us more about what made you hate Freddie Galloway in the first place, Mr Lucas,' Culverhouse said.

The solicitor interrupted. 'Is this line of questioning really necessary, Chief Inspector? My client has already told you that he no longer bore a grudge against Mr Galloway.'

'I think it is, yes,' Culverhouse replied. 'Because, let's face it, we only have your client's word for it that he's a reformed character.'

'His and that of the parole board,' Chamberlain added.

'Which, in my vast experience, can easily be swayed by a prisoner who knows how to say the right things. Which,' Culverhouse quickly added, to deflect the solicitor's obvious next remark, 'is not what I'm claiming your client has done, but does need to be considered as a possibility.'

Chamberlain looked at Lucas and nodded reluctantly.

Lucas sighed before speaking. 'He tucked me up. He tucked us all up in his own way. He knew damn well there was a far better escape route on that job. The one he took himself. The one he took, leaving me and Peter to face the music. And the time inside.'

'Peter being Benjamin Newell?' Wendy asked.

'If that's what your information tells you. I didn't know anyone's real names.'

'You knew Freddie Galloway's,' Culverhouse remarked.

'Only because you used his name first,' Lucas replied, after a moment or two.

'You named him when you were arrested over the Trenton-Lowe job. Then you retracted it.'

'I was scared. I was pressured into naming names. I got it wrong.'

'No you didn't. You knew exactly who we were talking about, didn't you?'

Lucas looked at his brief.

'Detective Chief Inspector, can we get onto the matter

of the crime itself? You've arrested my client for arson, yet all you seem to want to talk about is an event that happened eleven years ago and which seems to have no apparent connection to the crime you've arrested him for.'

Culverhouse looked at the solicitor and smiled. 'Certainly. Where were you on the evening of the nineteenth and early hours of the twentieth, John?'

'I was at home. My mother's old home. She left it to me. It's mine now.'

'Can anyone verify that?'

'What, that it's my home?'

Culverhouse eyed the man for a moment, letting him know silently that if anyone in this room was going to make cocky comments, it was going to be him.

'No, can anyone verify that you were there for the whole of last night?' Wendy asked.

'I live alone,' Lucas said, smiling slightly.

Culverhouse cocked his head. 'I don't know what you're smiling for, Mr Lucas. Your sworn enemy is killed in an arson attack hours after you get let out of prison – time you were serving for a job he abandoned you to get caught on – and you've got no alibi for the time of the attack. I don't think I'd be smiling if I were in your position.'

Lucas laughed. 'Why do you have this obsession with him being my "sworn enemy"? He was nothing of the sort. He was a bloke who fucked me over years ago. Shit happens. All that matters is how you deal with it.'

'And how did you deal with it?' Culverhouse asked him.

'I learned to forgive and forget. Prison gives you a lot of time to think.'

'And brood.'

Matthew Chamberlain, the solicitor, interjected. 'Detective Chief Inspector, the custody clock is ticking and so far we haven't got past you trying to convince my client that he was meant to hate Freddie Galloway. What, exactly, is the purpose of an interview if you're going to ignore everything he says and try to convince him otherwise?'

'Mr Chamberlain, I'm trying to get to the bottom of who set fire to Freddie Galloway's house, causing him to fall to his death. And, right now, circumstances are pointing heavily towards your client. That's why we're questioning him. That's our job.'

'Circumstances, Detective Chief Inspector. Circumstantial evidence. Nothing that will stand up in court, in other words.'

Culverhouse gritted his teeth. 'We've got officers searching Mr Lucas's property as we speak. Arresting him gives us the chance to speak to him under caution and question his version of events.'

'With respect, my client doesn't *have* a version of events. He's already told you he wasn't there. He was at his house, the house your officers are currently searching. God knows what for, seeing as he hadn't set foot in the place for eleven years until last night.'

'In which case, your client has nothing to worry about, does he?' Culverhouse replied. 'Unless, of course, the officers find some sort of forensic evidence that links to the events at Freddie Galloway's house. Now, that'd be a rather tricky one to explain, don't you think?'

Matthew Chamberlain looked at his client, who simply sat back in his chair and folded his arms.

19

It was often the case that the first custody interview with a suspect would seem completely fruitless. The general rule was that they'd either open up and tell you absolutely everything straight away or they'd frustrate you to the point where you wondered why you'd even bothered.

All wasn't lost, though. The team were coming to the end of their shift – or, at least, the end of the period of time they'd be allowed to work consecutively – save for the late debrief. Although historically murder investigations meant you worked whatever hours you could, this now had to be within a certain limit. After all, a wise defence solicitor could easily request staff working logs and claim that the investigation might be flawed in places due to overtired and overworked police officers. The truth of the matter was, all police officers were overtired and overworked regardless.

'Right,' Culverhouse said as he marched into the incident room, 'let's get this over and done with quickly. It's been a bloody long day and I've got a cold pint waiting for me next door. If we hurry up I might be able to drink it before closing time.'

Culverhouse sat down in a chair and folded his arms and legs, looking at Janet Grey expectantly.

The pathologist smiled, knowing the DCI's little ways only too well, and briefed the team on what she'd discovered so far.

'To summarise, it's pretty much what we expected when we first arrived at the scene. The cause of death was heavy trauma due to a fall, consistent with the height of the balcony and the weight of the deceased. It was the fall that killed him. There was quite a lot of smoke in his lungs, which indicates that he'd been inside the house when the fire was burning. There was no major evidence of scorching or any sign of him actively having tried to fight the fire, so we can assume that it was pretty well active by the time he discovered it.'

'Which is odd, isn't it?' Wendy asked. 'I mean, it makes sense that the fire had been well established by the time he discovered it, because it was during the night. He wouldn't have just been walking around the house at that time. But if that's the case, why didn't he die in his sleep of smoke inhalation? How did he discover the fire in the first place?'

'Fire alarms?' Steve offered, trying to hold back from laughing.

Wendy immediately felt rather daft. It had been a long day.

'Correct, DS Wing,' Dr Grey said. 'The watch commander reckons there are signs of smoke alarms having been installed, although it'll take a while for them to be able to confirm that for definite. Plastic doesn't tend to last too long in a blazing inferno, apparently. Who knew?'

'So what, he jumped and missed the pool?' Culverhouse asked.

'Looks like it. Probably not the easiest thing to do, especially if you've been woken in the middle of the night, are getting on a bit in age and you've got lungs half-filled with smoke. I'd like to see you land a perfect ten in the deep end, Detective Chief Inspector.'

'You're not the only one, Dr Grey. My body is a temple.'

'Yes. To Buddha.'

'Alright. Enough of the sexual tension. Let's get back to dead bodies. When are you going to have something I can use to charge our suspect?'

Janet Grey smiled. 'I'm afraid that's between science and the Crown Prosecution Service. I can't magic up evidence if it doesn't exist.'

Culverhouse grunted as he rubbed the stubble on his chin. 'No, but on the other hand the custody clock is ticking, and we're going to struggle to get an extension if there's nothing we can pin on our man. We can't interview again until the morning anyway. Not with Chamberlain as his brief. We're better off waiting until everyone's had some kip. Got to play well within the lines with that bloke.'

'Well, there's a first time for everything, eh, Detective

Chief Inspector?' Grey said, smiling at him as she closed her notebook.

'Have we had anything back from the scene?' Culverhouse asked, of no-one in particular.

'Nothing yet,' Steve Wing replied. 'But that doesn't mean they've not found anything. There's probably still some areas the fire officers won't let them into. Might take a while. They'll be going through the night, bagging and tagging.'

'Lucky them,' Culverhouse said. 'We'll need to hope they uncover something that ties our man to the scene. Otherwise, we'll have to release him.'

'That wouldn't be so bad, though, would it?' Ryan asked. 'I mean, he's got a probation officer assigned to him so it's not as if he's going to be able to go far.'

Culverhouse stood with his hands on his hips. 'Oh, I'm not worried about him going far. My concern is that if he's come out of prison and is exacting his revenge on people who've wronged him in the past, we have no idea how long that list of his might be. For all we know, he could be hell bent on knocking off as many old enemies as he can before we catch up with him. Which is why we need some sort of evidence either way, and pretty damn quickly.'

'They're doing their best,' Wendy said, trying to placate her boss. 'But as you say, there's not a whole lot we can do now other than head off and get some sleep.'

'Heh. Sleep? I'm having a pint. You lot coming?'

The DCI's tone of voice led them to believe it wasn't so

much an invitation as an order. And, in any case, each of them knew they could probably do with a drink.

20

Benjamin Newell stood, hands in his trouser pockets, a few feet behind the bench his new wife was sat on, watching as she gazed off at the treeline, the bottom of her flowing white dress resting on the grass.

The other guests had gone back inside, leaving the two of them to say whatever needed to be said. Lisa, however, didn't seem to be in the mood to say anything. He could tell everything from her face the moment he turned and saw her, the moment he realised she'd seen everything. In that split second, he'd realised he'd thrown it all away.

It had taken him years to prove to Lisa that he'd changed. Although she'd always said she trusted him and had faith in him, he knew the proof was in the pudding and she'd never be one hundred percent sure until he'd proven himself. And, in a few seconds of drunken madness, he'd undone all that hard work and lost everything he'd toiled for.

It certainly wasn't the way he'd envisaged his wedding day panning out. By now they were meant to be on the dance floor, sharing their first dance together as man and wife. Instead, they were out on the impressive lawn that led up to the venue, trying to work out what was going to happen to their fledgling marriage.

'I don't know what to say,' Benjamin said, as he took a few steps towards the bench.

'Don't say anything. And don't you dare come any closer,' Lisa said, her teeth gritted, not even bothering to turn and look at him.

He'd seen Lisa get angry and upset before – of course he had; he was no angel – but this was something completely different. There was an atmosphere that told him he'd ruined everything. There was a sense that he'd broken her trust, the faith she'd put in him in believing that he'd really changed, that he was no longer a bad person. To realise after all that the old Benjamin was still lurking beneath the surface somewhere must have hurt her enormously, he realised. He knew it had. It had hurt him, too.

'Lisa, I really don't know what happened. I've never been like that before, I promise. It's just... A few drinks, the emotion of the day, and then when he started... Look, I'm not making excuses. I'm just trying to make sense of it myself.'

Lisa shook her head and wiped her eyes. 'Sometimes you don't need to try making sense of things. They just are.'

'What's that meant to mean?'

'It doesn't need to mean anything. Leave me alone.'

Benjamin's shoulders sank. He knew he couldn't go back into the venue – not on his wedding day, with all his family and friends in there, most of whom would have now been told what had happened. Even if he managed to patch things up with Lisa he'd forever be the guy who started a fight on his own wedding day, the former criminal who never changed his ways and managed to suck a poor, innocent primary school teacher into the mix.

'Lisa, can I at least explain what was going through my head? I can completely see your point of view. I just want you to see mine.'

Benjamin heard what he thought sounded a bit like a laugh.

'I really don't think I want to know what's going through your mind. You led me to believe you'd changed. Four and a half years. What, were you just bottling it all up, waiting to get the ring on my finger so I couldn't change my mind? What happened? He was the first person you saw who you didn't like the look of, was he?'

Benjamin tried to stay composed and keep his voice calm. 'It wasn't like that at all. He was making... comments. Really lewd stuff, saying how he'd slept with you, talking about the stuff you'd done.'

Lisa kept looking off into the distance, but nodded slowly. 'And did he say when?'

'Before we met. When you started working at Sanderson Lees.'

'So, in other words, nothing to do with you.'

'That's not really how it works, Lisa. He–'

Lisa spun around on the bench to face him. 'No, that's exactly how it works. You had a life before me and I chose to ignore it and forgive it. How many people have I physically attacked because they mentioned something you'd done in your past? I'll tell you. None. Because I knew — I thought — you'd changed.'

'I have changed,' Benjamin said quietly.

'Yeah. Looks like it.'

Benjamin took a couple of steps closer to his wife. 'Lisa, that's not fair. I made one mistake. One mistake in four and a half years. You know how much I've changed, how different I am from the man I was before. I did one stupid thing. One. You can't hold that against me.'

Lisa stood up and walked over to Benjamin, her face neutral, until she was almost toe-to-toe, nose-to-nose with him.

He looked at her, her eyes darting back and forth between his as he tried to work out what she might be thinking.

After a few seconds of silence, she finally spoke. 'It was our wedding day. Our. Wedding day.'

And with that, she hitched up her dress and strode off back towards the venue.

Benjamin stood for a moment, staring into the space where Lisa had stood, trying his level best to get his head around what was happening. Was this it? Was she telling him it was all over, that he'd ruined it in front of all her family and friends? Was this going to go down as the shortest marriage in history?

Before he could torment himself too much about what had happened, his phone vibrated in his pocket; the familiar sound of a Formula 1 car zooming past as his chosen text tone. He pulled the phone out and glanced at the screen, seeing a text message from a number he didn't recognise – one that wasn't saved in his Contacts list. Regardless, he knew exactly who it was from based purely on the contents of the message.

He's out. We need to meet.

21

There was just enough time left before closing time at the Prince Albert for the team to grab a quick drink before heading off home for the night. Sometimes, a pint or a glass of wine was vital at the end of a long day.

Culverhouse had ordered a round of drinks and was busy trying to carry four glasses at once, whilst offering two banknotes to the barmaid with his teeth.

'Muchas gracias,' he said, as he clutched the glasses tightly, careful not to spill any liquid on the floor.

'What's your gut feeling on the Freddie Galloway case, then, guv?' Steve called out as Culverhouse made his way slowly towards the table.

'My feeling is you should keep your fucking voice down in the middle of the pub, Steve,' Culverhouse grunted. 'Do the words "active investigation" not mean anything to you?'

'Well there are only a couple of possibilities, aren't

there?' Steve said, now talking much more quietly, as Culverhouse dished out the drinks. 'I mean, there's the obvious theory that Lucas finally managed to get out and get his revenge. But he must've known he'd be the main suspect. Surely he wouldn't be that stupid.'

'Yeah well they don't call it "thick as thieves" for nothing,' Culverhouse remarked.

'What if he was being set up, though?'

'By who? He's just spent eleven years in the slammer.'

'We should try to remember that there's nothing actually tying Lucas to Galloway's death in any way, too. Not until forensics have reported back, and that won't be until the morning,' Wendy said.

'Yeah, well I've got a pile of cat shit in my back garden and I'm not blaming it on the sparrows,' Culverhouse said, taking a gulp of his pint. 'Speaking of which. Back in five,' he added, before standing and making his way to the toilet.

Ryan leaned forward and spoke quietly. 'What's up with him? He's even grumpier than usual.'

'Someone probably put milk in his coffee two weeks back,' Steve joked.

'Reckon it's anything to do with one of the others? I mean, Debbie went into his office to speak to him earlier and he's been pissed off ever since. Frank's gone straight home, too.'

'Frank's pretending he's semi-retired,' Wendy said. 'When in practice all that means is he works the same hours but just doesn't go to the pub afterwards.'

'It's not like Debbie not to join in, though,' Ryan said.

Wendy leaned in and spoke quietly. 'She's having a bit of trouble with her mum. She's ill, and lives down on the south coast somewhere. I'm not meant to say anything, so don't tell her I told you this. She reckons she might not have long left, so she's spending a lot of time down there when she's not working. I don't think that's enough, though.'

'Here, why'd she tell you that and not me?' Steve asked, seeming offended.

Wendy raised her eyebrows. 'I wonder.'

'Is that why he's pissed off?' Ryan asked.

Wendy took a sip of her drink. 'Possibly. I asked him about taking my inspectors' exams. I'd need to move some shifts around to do the exams and to prepare, and he turned it down. Even though it was his idea in the first place.'

'Can he even do that?'

'Course he can. Especially if it would be to the detriment of a case. You know what it's like here by now. With our staffing levels, even pausing to sneeze is to the detriment of a case.'

Ryan raised her eyebrows momentarily. 'I reckon he just needs to get laid.'

Wendy, almost choking on her drink, tried her best to convince Ryan that Jack Culverhouse and women didn't tend to mix well. 'His wife left him years back. Went abroad and took the daughter with her, apparently. Then she came back a year or two ago rattling with anti-depressants. Turns out the daughter never went anywhere and had been with his in-laws the whole time while she was off on her jollies. I hear the daughter is back living with him now, but this is all just hearsay. He never talks about any of it. I wish he would. It's clearly not doing him any good keeping it all bottled up.'

'Like I say, he just needs a good shag.'

'You offering?' Steve said, chipping in.

Wendy gave Steve a glance that told him that wasn't really the right thing to say.

'Not really my type,' Ryan replied. 'He's got one too many cocks for my liking.'

'Maybe you've just not met the right man yet. I reckon you could be turned.'

Wendy glanced at Steve again, hoping for his sake that Ryan wasn't the sort of woman who made complaints against colleagues.

'Even if that were true, I don't think Culverhouse would be the man to do it, do you?' Ryan replied, smiling at Wendy to let her know that she was taking this all in good jest. 'But seriously. Don't tell me we wouldn't all be better off if he had something else to occupy his spare time other than a bottle of Jack Daniel's and old re-runs of Minder. Plus it'd be fun watching it all happen.'

'Watching it? Jesus Christ, you're perverse,' Steve muttered, curling his upper lip.

'Not watching *that*, Steve. I mean setting him up with someone and watching it all unfurl. See what happens. Might make a nice psychological study at the very least. You know, we should set him up on one of those dating apps. There's loads of them. Gay ones, ones for people in uniform, ones for widowed pensioners. I'm sure there'll be one for overweight middle-aged bigots.'

'How the hell are you going to manage that?' Wendy asked, speaking quietly as she noticed Culverhouse walking back from the toilet.

Ryan smiled. 'Just watch and learn.'

22

Straight after he received the text message, Benjamin sent one of his own to both Lisa and Cameron.

Gone for a walk. Need to clear my head.

Once he was out of view of the wedding venue, he called the number that had sent him the text message. This was a conversation he didn't want to be having, but one he had always known was inevitable.

'Long time no speak,' came the familiar voice at the other end of the phone once the call had connected.

'How did you get this number?' Benjamin half-whispered half-barked.

'Alright, chill bruv. We got mutual friends, ain't we? Connections.'

Benjamin bit his lip hard, trying to hold his temper. 'We all agreed we were going our separate ways. Putting it behind us. And anyway, I've changed. I'm a new man now. I don't want anything to do with it.'

'You might not have much choice,' the voice at the other end said. 'You ain't heard, have you?'

Benjamin swallowed, fearing this was going to be something he didn't particularly want to hear. 'Heard what?'

'I can't tell you on the phone. Listen, meet me in the car park at the bottom of Mildenheath Common. How soon can you be there?'

'Uh, well I can call a cab. Depends when it turns up, but I'm probably ten, fifteen minutes away.'

'Right. Let's say half an hour. See you there.'

'Wait. What's this all ab—' Benjamin heard the call disconnect before he had a chance to ask his question. Tired, frustrated and stressed, he realised he wasn't going to be able to get out of this. He dialled the number of a local taxi company, the operator telling him someone would be with him in a few minutes.

Meanwhile, he perched on a low stone wall and considered how the hell his entire life had turned upside down in the space of half an hour. Earlier that night he'd been celebrating his wedding day with his nearest and dearest, over the moon that the woman he loved had vowed to stick with him in sickness and in health despite his chequered past, and now he was lamenting his broken marriage, sitting on a damp wall and waiting for a taxi to take him to a meeting he knew was going to be anything but fun.

. . .

Tyrone Golds got in his red Renault and drove the two miles to the car park at the foot of Mildenheath Common. It wasn't somewhere he usually went all that often, but he knew it was secluded and free of CCTV cameras. It wouldn't do for them to be seen meeting. Not now.

He'd called Benjamin Newell, who he remembered as Peter, from a burner phone – an unregistered pay-as-you-go mobile he'd got from one of the lads at the boxing club. The police wouldn't connect him with this number and there was no way they'd be tracing Peter's calls, either. Tyrone knew the guy had been clean for years.

Knowledge of their meeting getting out wouldn't necessarily cause either of them any issues, but it still wasn't a risk he wanted to take.

Because, after all, it wasn't the police he was afraid of.

'Just drop me off at the end of the road here, mate,' Benjamin said, as he pulled his wallet out of his inside jacket pocket.

The taxi driver had been far too chatty for his liking, asking all sorts of questions. Whose wedding was it? A friend's, he told him. He'd been an usher. Why was he going home already? His kid was ill, he said. Had to get home to see him. How old's the kid? What's his name? In the end, Benjamin had made an excuse about feeling unwell and said he'd walk the rest of the way, told the driver he needed the fresh air.

He wasn't technically lying.

Having paid his ten quid and half-walked half-jogged towards the car park, he could feel the butterflies in his stomach as his legs started to feel like jelly beneath him. He knew from Tyrone's voice that this wasn't going to be good news. He knew it would be something that would turn his whole life upside down and drag him right back to where he was all those years ago, long before he met Lisa.

When he got to the car park, he could see there was only one car in there. There was a man sat in the driver's seat. He couldn't see who it was at first, but as he got closer he recognised Tyrone Golds, the man who he'd known as Bruno. He'd barely changed in all that time. He'd kept in shape, presumably by keeping up the boxing, and looked a good ten years younger than he was.

Benjamin got in the passenger seat and closed the door behind him.

'Years have been mean to you, bruv,' Tyrone said, looking at him.

Well fuck you too, Benjamin thought, regretting noticing how young Tyrone looked. 'Sign of a life well lived,' he said. 'No-one's gonna admire anyone's perfect skin from six feet under.'

'Yeah, well you ain't so far from the truth,' Tyrone said, shuffling in his seat. 'With the six feet under bit, I mean. Freddie Galloway's dead. Someone set fire to his fucking house.'

Benjamin's heart started thudding in his chest. This was bringing back memories he'd tried hard to suppress. He'd spent the last eleven years trying to forget about Footloose Freddie and the bungled job, and now meeting Tyrone and just hearing the mention of Freddie Galloway's name had ruined it all in a heartbeat. 'What? Who?' he asked.

'No-one knows. But they're sure as hell sniffing around.'

'Wait. Your text. It said "He's out". What did you mean?'

Tyrone shook his head. 'What do you think I meant? I meant Headache, bruv. He's out. Been released. And get this: he was let out yesterday morning. Few hours later, Footloose is lying on his back patio like a fucking burnt kebab. You telling me that ain't linked? That ain't no coincidence, I'm telling you.'

Benjamin tried to calm his thoughts and process this information. 'So what are you saying? That he's going to come after us?'

Tyrone shrugged and cocked his head slightly. 'Your guess is as good as mine. All I know is if that guy's on the fucking warpath we ain't gonna be far from his sights.'

'But why? We didn't do anything wrong. I was there with him, I tried to stop him pulling that trigger. I went with him while you and Footloose ran over the fucking hills for freedom.'

'You fucked off the second he fired that gun, bruv. Left him to it just the same as we did. He's been behind bars for nearly eleven years. You know what that does to a man? Sends them insane, that's what. Every second of every day, thinking about it. Just thinking about it. Ain't no amount of exercise time or creative writing classes gonna stop your mind from messing with you in that place.'

Benjamin swallowed. 'And if it wasn't him?'

'Well if it wasn't him, we're really in the shit. 'Cos then the filth are gonna come sniffing around us, you get me? We all got shafted by Freddie Galloway, bruv. All of us.'

Benjamin shook his head. 'But we've had eleven years to do something about that. Why would we wait until the day Headache's released and do it then?'

Tyrone's voice took on an edge of anger. 'Because the moment he pulled that fucking trigger, that changed everything. You know, ever since that day I've been shitting myself. Headache could've coughed at any minute and told the cops who else was involved. Could've cut a deal and got his sentence reduced. But he didn't. Now, that's either because he's a fucking God's honest geezer or because he knew he was better off biding his time. And even if it's because he's Mother fucking Teresa reincarnated, it's not just him we had to worry about. I know we were careful, but you know damn well our DNA'll still be all over that place. Do you know what it's like to be a black guy driving around a town like this, knowing you're God knows how many times more likely to be pulled over by the cops than a white guy like you? And that if they do a cheek swab, or whatever damn DNA test they want, I'll be going down for armed robbery just because I forgot to indicate at a fucking roundabout?'

Benjamin knew the feeling all too well, but he didn't feel that was something he could tell Tyrone right now.

'So if one of us is meant to have burnt Freddie Galloway's place down, why would either of us risk leaving our DNA there too? If we were that worried about being caught for armed robbery, why would we throw arson and murder in the mix?'

'That's what I've been thinking too. And it came to me that that might be just the sort of thing someone would do if they wanted to frame Headache. If they wanted to make it look like it was him, getting revenge the same day he got out of prison. If they wanted to make sure he'd keep his mouth shut.'

'But I don't get it,' Benjamin said. 'I don't get why either of us would do that.'

Tyrone held Benjamin's gaze for a little longer than Benjamin would've liked.

'Nor do I, bruv. Nor do I.'

23

'Come on, just one more,' Ryan said, standing to take the empty glasses to the bar. 'We're all having one.'

'You've all got to be in at eight tomorrow morning,' Culverhouse said, starting to slur slightly. 'And so have I.'

'And we will. That's hours away yet. Anyway, call it a team bonding exercise. Besides, you'll have to leave the car at work anyway now, so the walk home and back again in the morning will sort you right out.'

Culverhouse let out a grunt that told Ryan he didn't necessarily agree but wasn't going to argue.

With another round of drinks on the table, and thanks given to the landlord for letting them stay well beyond last orders, Ryan wasted no time in getting to the point.

'A friend of mine was in here the other night,' she said, taking a sip of her drink. 'He went on a date from one of those apps.'

Ryan, Wendy and Steve tried to look at Culverhouse to

gauge his reaction without making it too obvious they were watching him. He didn't seem to be responding at all, but was watching the flashing lights on the fruit machine near the toilets.

'Yeah? How did it go?' Steve asked, sounding suspiciously enthusiastic.

'Well, he didn't go back to his that night if that's what you're asking,' Ryan said, squirming as Steve belted out an elongated, forced laugh.

Culverhouse looked at him. 'What the fuck's wrong with you?'

'Me? Nothing. Why?'

'No reason. Just remind me not to order whatever that is you're drinking.'

'You ever been on one of those?' Ryan asked Culverhouse, while his attention was back on the table.

'One of what?'

'Dating apps. I was just saying a friend of mine's on one and he's ploughing through the town like Don Juan.'

Culverhouse raised his eyebrows. 'Good for him. Should keep the local STD clinic in business.'

'Ah, come on. It's only a bit of fun, isn't it?' Wendy chipped in.

Culverhouse looked at her, cocking his head slightly. 'Are you on them?'

Wendy tried to work out the subtext of his question, but she couldn't. Instead, she decided to answer honestly. 'Me? No.'

'Have you seriously never tried them?' Ryan asked him.

'Obviously not,' the DCI replied. 'Why would I?'

'Because that's how things are done nowadays, isn't it? You don't need to worry about going out to places and hoping that someone you're attracted to turns up at the same place at the same time and wants to talk to you. You just browse through, see who takes your fancy and either swipe left or right.'

Culverhouse took a large gulp of his beer. 'Sounds like a fucking Argos catalogue.'

Ryan considered this for a moment. 'Yeah, if you like. And if the same person sees your profile and likes you too, they swipe the same way and it pops up as a match.'

'Then what?' Culverhouse asked, starting to sound vaguely interested.

'Then you can send them a message. Get chatting, find out a bit more about each other, meet up if you want to. It's ideal for people who are busy with work and don't get to go out and socialise and meet new people.' She watched Culverhouse for a reaction, but got none. 'Here, give me your phone and I'll show you.'

'Bugger off, use yours,' Culverhouse replied.

'I can't do that, can I? I've got a partner. Wouldn't look too good if I was on dating apps.'

Culverhouse sat back and folded his arms. 'Yeah, well I don't particularly fancy people spotting me on there either.'

'Why not? Almost every person in the country who's single is on them. Guaranteed. And anyway, you can set it so certain people can't see you. You can change the settings so only women of a certain age can see your profile, or people from a specific geographical area. It's safe. Believe me.'

The DCI narrowed his eyebrows. 'How do you know?'

'I'm twenty-five,' Ryan replied, chuckling. 'It's how things are done these days. Seriously, just pass me your phone and I'll show you. You don't have to make your profile public or anything. I'll just show you how it works.'

Culverhouse, sensing he wasn't going to get any peace, fished his phone out of his pocket and slid it across the table towards Ryan.

'What's the unlock code?' Ryan asked, before picking up the phone.

'The what now?'

'The unlock code. The pin number.'

Culverhouse shook his head. 'Haven't got one.'

'They always say coppers are the worst with security,' Steve remarked.

Once Ryan had downloaded and installed the app on Culverhouse's phone, she opened it up and started to configure it. 'How tall are you?' she asked.

Culverhouse shrugged.

'Shall we say six foot? Most women wouldn't go for anything under. Sorry Steve. Right. Hobbies and interests. Minimum of fifty characters.'

'How many letters in "fuck all"?'

Ryan laughed. 'Not enough. Shall I put travelling and seeing the world, good food, fine wine, great company?'

Culverhouse snorted. 'Women like six-foot liars, do they?'

'It's not about lying. It's about making a good first impression.'

'By lying.'

'By bending the truth slightly. Now. A picture. Sit back, look relaxed and smile.'

Steve let out a huge belly laugh. 'Hah! Smile! Talk about breaking new horizons.'

'Fuck off, Steve,' Culverhouse replied, before leaning back in his chair, casually draping his arm over the one next to him and forcing the most awkward looking grin any of them had ever seen.

Wendy tried her hardest not to laugh, and instead buried her face in her drink.

'Yeah, try not to force it,' Ryan said. 'Just relax your face and think of something that made you really happy.'

Culverhouse seemed to pause for a moment, before finding something in his memory bank. The smile seemed warm and genuine, and left Wendy wondering what could have been the thought that went through his mind at that moment.

'Lovely,' Ryan said. 'That looks great.'

'Now what?'

'Now we get swiping.'

24

John Lucas stretched and arched his back as he adjusted to the light streaming into his cell. He'd had a better night's sleep than he had any right to, sleeping on a tough plastic mattress in a cold prison cell. Then again, he'd got used to waking up to whitewashed brick walls and the clanging of metal doors down a corridor. He hadn't expected to ever have to hear it again, though.

The hatch in the door slid open as a police officer unlocked it and looked in on him.

'Not dead,' Lucas called out, raising his hand.

'Always a bonus,' said the officer. 'Saves me a ton of paperwork. You want breakfast?'

'I'll pass if that's alright. I'm still recovering from dinner. Wouldn't mind a cup of tea, though.'

'Right you are. They'll probably call down for you just before nine, to get you in for interviewing again.'

Lucas nodded and put his head back down on the hard

mattress. With any luck, the custody clock would run down and he'd be out of here within a couple of hours. He hoped so. Because he had places to be.

Despite two bacon sandwiches and three cups of black coffee, Jack Culverhouse could still feel and taste his hangover. It was something most CID officers got used to with time — there was fun to be had trying to work out which symptoms were due to the drink and which were down to sleep deprivation.

'Morning, guv!' Steve Wing bellowed, whilst giving Culverhouse a firm but friendly slap on the back. 'Got some good news for you.'

'Unless you're being transferred to the Outer fucking Hebrides, I fail to see how it could brighten up my morning,' Culverhouse replied.

'Well, you never know. I took a call from the search teams about ten minutes ago. They've got an update on what they've found.'

Culverhouse squinted as he tried to force the splitting headache to the back of his skull. 'Go on.'

'From the scene, not much. The fire was pretty intense, but all they can say for definite is that the fire started by the front door. They reckon it was done with petrol and a hosepipe with a length of thin rope running through it. Acts as a wick, apparently, and means the person doing it can avoid scorching themselves. Makes it forensically more difficult to link someone to the scene.'

'So is there anything linking Lucas to it? Or are you just wasting my time?' Culverhouse barked.

'See, that's where it gets interesting,' Steve said. 'There was nothing at the scene as such, but when they searched Lucas's home they found a few things that might interest you.'

Culverhouse was, by now, starting to lose what little patience he still had. 'Steve, will you fucking spit it out?'

'Shoes. They managed to gain access to Lucas's garage, which had a pretty hefty lock on it. There was a pair of shoes in there – size nine, same as Lucas wears – with some mud and grass on the bottom of them. They reckon the type of grass is the same as on Freddie Galloway's front lawn, and the mud is a pretty close match too.'

'Pretty close?'

'Eighty-five percent, they reckon. Could be because the shoes have been worn elsewhere and have been contaminated with a couple of different types of mud. Dunno how it'd stand up in court, but to be honest it might not need to. They also found a jerry can with traces of petrol in the bottom of it. They're doing analysis on it as we speak, trying to confirm whether it was the same petrol used in the fire. Depends what they can extract from the burnt remains of the house. But that's not all. The fire officers reckon the curtains and soft furnishings near the front door were splashed with accelerant too, meaning the arsonist would've likely needed to have access to the house. Amongst all the tools and stuff in his garage drawers, they found a key.

Looks pretty new. They've confirmed it matches the lock on Galloway's front door.'

'He had a key to Galloway's house?'

'Looks like it. There are no prints on the key or the jerry can, but that's hardly a surprise. There are traces of latex dust which match a box of gloves found in Lucas's garage.'

'Excellent. Any DNA on the shoes?'

'Nothing so far. They've managed to get some cotton fibres, probably from the socks he wore, but no hairs or skin fragments or anything like that. You'd expect to find something, but looks like he was careful. There was even latex dust on the laces, showing he likely tied them up whilst wearing the gloves.'

'Fantastic. Really good work, Steve,' Culverhouse said, slapping him on the back twice as hard as the Detective Sergeant had done to him a few moments ago. 'Right. Where's Knight?'

'Gone to fetch something from the printer upstairs.'

'Did you tell her about the forensics?'

'Yeah, she was here when the call came in. We wanted to wait until you arrived before doing anything, though. Thought you might want to take the lead on this one.'

'Send her down to the custody suite when she gets back, will you? I think it's about time we had another little chat with Mr Lucas.'

25

Once Wendy had joined Culverhouse down in the custody suite, they entered the interview room, where John Lucas was already waiting, sitting alongside his solicitor, Matthew Chamberlain.

'Morning all,' Culverhouse said. 'Lovely weather out there, isn't it?'

'I wouldn't know,' Lucas replied, before his brief could advise him otherwise.

'Well, maybe after we've had a little chat you'll be able to pop out for a bit. I wouldn't bank on it, though.'

'Before we start, Detective Chief Inspector,' the solicitor said, 'would you mind fetching me another cup of coffee, please? This one's got sugar in it.'

'Tough,' Culverhouse said, before starting the recording equipment and introducing the people present in the room.

'Mr Lucas. Have you ever visited the house of one Frederick Galloway?'

'No. I haven't.'

'You weren't close to Mr Galloway? You didn't go round and water his plants or feed his cats while he was away on holiday?'

Lucas looked at his solicitor, who responded by talking to Culverhouse.

'Where is this line of questioning going, exactly, Detective Chief Inspector?'

Culverhouse furrowed his brow and looked back at the brief. 'Your client responding to it, with any luck, Mr Chamberlain. They're fairly simple questions.'

Chamberlain nodded at Lucas.

'No. I've never been to his house.'

'What's your shoe size, Mr Lucas?' Culverhouse asked, keeping his eyes on the notepad in front of him.

'Nine.'

'And do you own a pair of size nine Timberland boots?'

'Uh, I dunno. Possibly. I've been in prison for the past decade; I don't remember what brands of shoes I've got sitting in my wardrobe.'

'What about your garage?' Culverhouse asked, looking up at him. He saw no sign of recognition, other than a glint of surprise in the man's eyes.

'My garage?'

'Yes, that brick structure attached to the side of your house, traditionally used to store a car but nowadays more often used for storing tools and garden equipment. And size nine Timberland boots.'

Lucas shook his head. 'I've no idea. I've not been in the garage since before I went to prison.'

'Can you prove that?'

Lucas laughed. 'Funnily enough, no. It's not the sort of thing I jotted down in my diary if that's what you mean.'

'So you can't explain why there's a pair of size nine Timberland boots sitting in your garage, the bottoms of which are covered in mud and blades of grass that have been matched to Freddie Galloway's front lawn?'

Culverhouse watched as Lucas sat in a stunned silence for a few moments, seeming to hold his breath the whole time.

'Can I have a couple of minutes with my client, please?' Chamberlain asked.

'You can have as long as it takes me to get myself another cup of coffee,' Culverhouse replied, before stating the time and pausing the recording equipment.

Back outside the interview room, he asked Knight what she made of Lucas's responses.

'I dunno. He seemed genuinely shocked,' she said. 'I don't imagine that's because he seriously thought he'd get away with hiding stuff like that in the garage, so my instinct is that he genuinely knew nothing about it.'

'Doesn't quite add up, though, does it?'

'It does if someone was trying to set him up.'

Culverhouse nodded and scratched at his stubbly chin. 'True. Wouldn't hurt to run along that line of questioning for a bit, see who might have wanted to frame him for it. When we go back in, you can take over the questioning. See if you can get something else out of him. People always tend to open up more to birds.'

'Birds?' Wendy asked, raising her eyebrows, even though she hadn't taken any serious offence to the remark.

'Call it good-cop bad-cop. Call it what you like. All I know is these ex-cons and gangsters will try to run circles round you if you let them. We need to keep switching things up, keep dropping things on them. Sooner or later, he'll talk. He'll either tell us what he's done — or the evidence will — or he'll cough about who he's tucked up in the past. Either way, we'll get our man.'

Once both detectives were suitably dosed up on more black coffee, they re-entered the interview room and started the recording equipment running again. They said nothing other than to confirm the recommencement of the interview, then sat and looked at John Lucas.

'Sorry, did you have a question for my client?' Matthew Chamberlain asked, his tone of voice beginning to rile Culverhouse.

'He still hasn't answered my last one yet,' the DCI chipped in, seemingly forgetting their agreement to allow Wendy to do the talking. 'What was a pair of size nine Timberland boots doing in your garage, with mud and grass from Freddie Galloway's front lawn all over them?'

Lucas looked at his solicitor before speaking. 'I don't know.'

'Not really an answer, is it?' Culverhouse asked, before Wendy nudged him under the table and began talking.

'Mr Lucas, we do conduct forensic tests on these sorts of items. We'll be able to tell conclusively whether you wore those boots.' Wendy watched as Lucas digested this information, although she didn't let on that the tests had already come back negative. If he was the arsonist, he'd still be panicking, not knowing how the test results would come back. If he was clean, he'd be delighted to hear about the tests, knowing they could prove his innocence.

'Like I said. I don't remember half of what I had before I went inside. It was a long time ago.'

'These boots are new. They were only released four years ago.'

'Well there you go, then,' Lucas said. 'Can't have been mine, can they? I was inside.'

'All that means is you didn't pop down to the shop and buy them yourself. Did your mum buy them? A friend? Acquaintance, perhaps? They look pretty new. Maybe someone was getting you set up with some new stuff before you were released.'

'Like who? I haven't got anyone. If you've found a pair of new boots in my garage, they're not mine.'

Wendy leaned forward as she spoke. 'See, that's not all we found in your garage. We also found a jerry can with traces of petrol in the bottom of it. The fire officers believe petrol was used to start the fire at Freddie Galloway's house. They're working on tests as we speak to see if they're from the same batch. We also found a key to Freddie

Galloway's house. To the front door, which we know the arsonist had access to, to douse the soft furnishings with petrol – petrol found in the bottom of a jerry can in your garage. The shoes, jerry can and key had traces of latex dust on them – dust which matches a box of latex gloves found in your garage. Do you have any comment on that?'

John Lucas buried his head in his forearms on the desk, but said nothing.

'Detective Sergeant, let me ask you a question,' Matthew Chamberlain said. 'If you suppose that my client went to all that effort to remain forensically clean by wearing latex gloves, not handling the jerry can or boots without them on, buying a new pair of boots so none of his were traced to the scene, why on earth would he store all those incriminating items in his own garage? He would have known he'd be the first person you'd call on, especially considering his past and the fact that he'd only got out of prison hours earlier. Do you really think he'd make such a huge number of schoolboy errors?'

'I have no idea what was going through your client's mind at the time, Mr Chamberlain, nor how good he is at hiding evidence. All I know is that we found those items in his garage and that the finger of suspicion points firmly at him. I'm simply asking for his comment on that.'

'I have nothing to say,' John Lucas said, eventually.

There was silence for a few moments before Culverhouse spoke. 'Who are you covering up for, John?'

'Detective Chief Inspector, make your mind up. Are you accusing my client of arson or covering up for–'

'I'm trying to get to the bottom of who set fire to Freddie Galloway's house, who caused him to have to jump from a second-floor window to save his own life, a jump which failed spectacularly. Those items were found in your client's garage. Like it or not, he was involved somehow. He either did it, covered up for someone who did it, or is being set up by the person who did it. Either way, we're going to get to the truth and it'll be a lot better for your client if he cooperates.'

'With respect, Detective Chief Inspector, if he's being set up by someone else I think you'll agree my client then becomes the victim. So why is he sitting in an interview room in the custody suite, being grilled by you two? If you can't come up with some conclusive evidence that my client has even set foot in that garage since being released from prison, you might as well save your time and ours by releasing him right now.'

Culverhouse looked at Chamberlain for a few moments before smiling. 'We'll be in touch,' he said, before ending the recording and gesturing for Wendy to follow him out of the room.

'Are you going to release him, then?' Wendy asked.

'No, I'm going to bail him. How long's left on the custody clock?'

'Erm. His twenty-four hours runs out in an hour and a quarter.'

'Right. Get him bailed right on the fucking dot. Not a second earlier. And next time that bastard Chamberlain asks for a coffee, give him eight fucking sugars.'

26

Tyrone took off his t-shirt and replaced it with a vest. The problem with this flat — as well as all the other downsides to it — was that it was freezing cold for half the year and roasting hot for the rest of it. He couldn't even open the windows as far as he'd like, thanks to the council installing some sort of device that meant people couldn't fall or jump out of them. He stood by the window and sipped at the air it allowed in through the small gap.

He didn't have to take a training session until four in the afternoon, which'd give him plenty of time to chill, even though that was the wrong word to use in this heat. It was no wonder so many kids spent their days wandering around the estate, hanging around on street corners. Even in the height of summer and the blazing sun, it was still cooler out there than it was in the damn flats.

Tyrone wouldn't have minded living there on his own. It had started to get a bit cramped the more Shanice's boyfriend, Elijah, had come to stay. That happened more and more often as their relationship grew, but once Shanice fell pregnant they'd tried their best to move out and get their own place. That hadn't been as easy as they'd hoped, though, with the council telling them they already had a perfectly good home. They'd been on the waiting list for a new place ever since, but didn't hold out much hope of ever getting to the top. Those places would always go to people who were homeless or facing eviction. As much as Tyrone loved his nephew Caleb, living in the same small flat as a screaming baby and his sister's boyfriend wasn't his idea of fun.

Caleb was nearly two, now, and — fair play to them — Shanice and Elijah were still going strong. Tyrone'd had his doubts about the guy at first, but he couldn't deny that he gave Shanice the stability and purpose she needed. Other girls in her position could've easily gone off the rails at any point. He'd seen it happen too many times on the estate already.

He'd often wondered whether Shanice's occasional remarks about him getting a girlfriend of his own had been laced with some sort of knowingness. They say women have some sort of in-built radar, don't they? Almost like an early warning system. *Whoa! No, not that one. Don't waste your time!* Were his sister's comments her way of trying to encourage him to confirm what she'd always believed, always known? Or maybe she was genuinely interested, wondering when her younger brother was going to settle down with a girlfriend of his own.

Either way, she'd be disappointed. He wasn't going to settle down with a girl. Sure, he could find a woman and go through the usual rituals but what would be the point? He'd be lying to her and to himself. Who would benefit, other than the perverse estate logic that being gay was somehow a sign of weakness, a thing to be ashamed of? He didn't want any part of that. But at the same time, there was no way he was ever going to live anywhere else. He didn't have the means to do so, nor the inclination to feel he should have to run away from who he was.

Fortunately for him, though, it had remained his secret. As long as it continued like that, he was comfortable enough.

The biggest problem in his life right now was going to be the man who'd certainly lived up to his name over the past couple of days: Headache.

He had no idea how this was going to play out, and he didn't want to try to guess either. All he knew was the general consensus had been that the group would all go their separate ways, never speak to anyone about the bungled robbery and ensure that the police had nothing else to work with. Sure, people had been caught and others had got away. But that was life, right? They all collectively had too much to lose if someone decided to act up, blab their mouth or try and get some sort of revenge.

But then they weren't just dealing with your general, run-of-the-mill people here. These were criminals who'd happily double-cross a friend for a wad of cash, not think twice about setting each other up if it meant there was a chance they'd be able to get one step ahead of someone else. Is that the sort of thing Peter would do? Wait all those years for Headache to be released, only to tuck him up by making it look like he'd burnt down Freddie Galloway's house? He doubted it, but then again you couldn't put anything past people like that.

Tyrone buttered a slice of toast and tried to forget all about Freddie Galloway, life on the estate and everything else for a few moments. Life tended to throw him these curveballs from time to time, but he was an expert hitter. He'd find a way of smashing this one out of the park, too.

As he crunched down on the slice of toast and wiped the smeared butter from his top lip, he heard the sound of paper sliding under the front door to the flat. It wasn't an unfamiliar sound. Although the mailboxes were all downstairs near the front entrance to the block, it wasn't uncommon for people to gain access to the corridors and put leaflets and mailers under the doors. It was usually something to do with a neighbourhood watch meeting or some sort of council application for redeveloping land. The sort of stuff that went straight in the recycling bin.

But Tyrone could see straight away, even from this distance, that this sheet of paper was very different. He walked over to the front door, bent down and picked up the folded A4 sheet, trying not to get butter on it as he unfolded it.

There was a message written on it, in landscape, spelt out with letters cut out from old newspapers and magazines, much like the stereotypical ransom note in a bad film. But this was no ransom note. This was a threat.

Tyrone swallowed hard, his heart hammering in his chest as he read the message again.

I FUCKIN KILL U QUEER POOF

This was more than just a threat. This was someone trying to tell him they knew his secret.

Before he could think about what he was doing, he unlocked the door, flung it back against the wall and went running down the corridor, before leaning over the stairs and looking down into the stairwell. He could see nothing. He took the stairs three or four at a time, bouncing down them at rapid speed, before getting to the bottom floor. The front door was closed. He opened it and stepped outside, looking left and right and across the street, but he could see nothing. Nothing but the same old tired estate he'd always known.

27

'Here's a question,' Wendy said, as she watched the traffic lights turn from amber to red. 'Why not apply for an extension on John Lucas? We could've kept him in for longer that way.'

'And what's the point?' Culverhouse said, drumming his fingers on the steering wheel. 'It's all circumstantial. We can't prove he put any of that stuff there – the house didn't have anyone living in it after his mum died. Anyone could've gained access and put those things in his garage. Something doesn't feel right. I can't quite put my finger on it.'

'I can. It's all too convenient. Like his brief said, why would he do something like that hours after getting out of prison, then leave a load of clues pointing to him? He's had years to think about this and plan it.'

Culverhouse stayed silent for a few moments. 'What I don't get is his attitude in that interview room. He wasn't exactly playing the innocent, was he? He was almost acting as if it was some sort of game, as if he was playing us.'

'To be fair, he's spent the last decade inside. I don't imagine he's got the highest opinion of police officers, nor did he expect to be in an interview room again the day after coming out of prison.'

'Well, if he didn't expect it, that tells me he didn't do it,' Culverhouse replied.

Wendy had to agree her hunch was similar, although that didn't help them come any closer to identifying who did set fire to Freddie Galloway's house.

Interviewing victims of historic crimes was never pleasant at the best of times. It invariably either resulted in not very much information being uncovered at all due to the passage of time, or it opened up old wounds for the victim, leaving the questioning officers feeling guilty for having to drag up old dirt again.

This time, though, they knew it was going to be even more difficult. Owen McCready had been one of them, a police officer who'd made the honest mistake of responding to an emergency call all those years ago. He'd been the closest officer to the scene at the time, so had been the first man there. His real downfall, though, had been his photographic memory and eye for detail. Remembering and identifying John Lucas at the scene of the robbery had resulted in him being repaid with a bullet in the skull.

Neither of them said a word as they pulled up outside Owen McCready's house. It was a sorry state of affairs — a decent house which had no doubt been covered by the financial payout he and his family would've received on discovering he couldn't work again, adorned with a bright white plastic handrail on the outside wall and a ramp up to the front door. It was the unfortunate sign of an honourable man who'd been in the wrong place at the wrong time.

Owen's wife, Cassandra, took Wendy and Jack through to the living room, where Owen was already seated in an armchair.

'I can walk with help most of the time,' he said, as if feeling he had to excuse being immobile. 'Sometimes even on my own, but it's not as smooth as it used to be. On bad days, I get excruciating headaches and need a chair to get around. Something to do with swelling on the brain. It comes and goes.'

The two officers looked at each other, the unspoken words being that this could easily have been either of them, or any other officer they knew. Someone who'd been gunned down doing his job, and had his life ruined as a result.

'I hope you don't mind us asking you to go over old ground,' Wendy said, knowing damn well that Owen McCready must think about those events every single day of his life.

'No, it's fine. I had a call to say John Lucas was being released the other day. I presume it didn't take him long to go back to his old ways.'

'We don't know,' Wendy said, with a large exhalation of breath. 'There's been a crime committed which involves somebody linked with the Trenton-Lowe incident. There's a possibility it could involve one or more of the people involved.'

'And is Lucas your suspect or victim?'

Wendy looked at Jack, unsure how much information she should divulge. 'Suspect,' she said, eventually.

'Never mind.'

She guessed she couldn't blame him for feeling like that. 'Now, I know from your statements at the time that you said the only person you recognised was John Lucas. Has anything else come to mind since you made those statements?'

Owen shook his head slowly. 'No, nothing. I mean, I know one of the other guys was called Benjamin Newell. But that's only because the silly twat got himself arrested shortly after. I'd never heard the name before then, and I didn't recognise him. They reckon there was four, don't they?'

'According to the security guard inside the building, yes,' Wendy said. 'But I'm afraid we can't go to him. He took his own life a few weeks after the court case.'

'Ah. I didn't know that. No-one told me. Sounds a bit suspicious, doesn't it?'

'Possibly so. But the coroner ruled it was suicide.'

'Convenient,' Owen said, looking at the wall.

Wendy had the impression that Owen was a man who had become quite bitter about what had happened to him. She supposed she couldn't blame him. It couldn't be easy having your whole life turned upside down by one idiot with a gun. Owen was a victim of circumstance. A man who'd always tried his best, but one time tried too hard.

'And you've not had any strange goings on? No messages, weird noises outside, nothing like that?' Wendy asked.

'No. Nothing. But then again I don't see why I would. The only one I identified was Lucas, and he never had any venom towards me. He held his hatred for Freddie Galloway. He was furious that even though he'd initially blabbed Galloway's name, they'd never been able to prove he was involved. He felt the police had done him over. Galloway knew he'd been identified by Lucas, and Lucas got nothing out of it other than a lengthy jail sentence. He put his faith in the police that they'd find enough to charge Galloway too and reduce Lucas's sentence for cooperation. Don't get me wrong, I hope they reserve a special place in hell for the guy, but I can see why he'd be pissed off.'

Wendy and Jack exchanged another look. Whichever way they turned, it seemed, the web of intrigue and vortex of vengeance seemed to get only fiercer and more confusing.

Once they realised they'd got all there was to get out of Owen McCready, they said their goodbyes and left. Just as Culverhouse was about to start the car up, his mobile phone started ringing. Frank Vine's number was on the screen.

'Frank,' Culverhouse barked.

'Guv, we just had an interesting call come through on the main switchboard. A guy asking to speak to the senior investigating officer looking into the Freddie Galloway case.

His words, not mine. He says he's got some information that could help.'

'Right. What's his name?'

'He wouldn't say.'

Culverhouse blinked a few times. Time wasters were common on major investigations, but they usually got weeded out at the first line of defence. 'What do you mean he wouldn't say?'

'He said he wants to meet you anonymously in a café in town. Just my own personal hunch here, but I reckon someone's leaning on him. He sounded more afraid of giving too much away than anything, but seemed keen to talk.'

Culverhouse mulled this over for a minute. If the guy wanted to meet in a café, it was unlikely to be an ambush. At the worst, it could just be a timewaster.

'When does he want to meet?'

'Now. He's on his way to Café Fresco. Said he'll wait there an hour or so. He sounded like he was pretty desperate to speak to someone.'

Culverhouse looked at his watch. He could be there in ten or fifteen minutes.

'Right. Okay then. How am I meant to know who I'm meeting, though?'

'Uh, good point,' Frank said. 'He sounded black, if that helps.'

Culverhouse closed his eyes and shook his head. 'Yeah. Thanks Frank. Thanks a bunch.'

28

They'd arranged for Wendy to go into the coffee shop a minute or so ahead of Jack, and to grab a drink and sit at another table – just in case. As Culverhouse entered the café, he noticed the only black man in the room was sitting towards the back, looking nervous.

He strode over and stopped at the table. 'You my date for the evening?'

'If you're the guy in charge, yeah,' the man said, standing up to shake his hand.

'Jack Culverhouse.'

'Uh, Ty.'

'Ty? What's that short for? Bear in mind I'm going to need to know your full name at some point anyway.'

The man sat back down and wrung his hands. Culverhouse sat down opposite him.

'Do you want a coffee or something?' Tyrone asked.

'Nope.'

'What about tea?'

'No. I don't want anything other than for you to tell me what this is about.'

Tyrone nodded. 'Right. I just dunno where to start, you know? It ain't easy. All I know is something ain't right.'

Culverhouse rolled his eyes. 'Lots of things "ain't right". It "ain't right" that there's war and suffering in the world. It "ain't right" that I can't get the foil lid off a Pot Noodle without leaving a little bit stuck the rim. It "ain't right" that I'm sitting here when I should be busy running a major investigation.'

'That's what I wanted to talk to you about,' Tyrone said, leaning forward.

'Go on.'

Tyrone took a deep breath before speaking. 'I know someone torched Freddie Galloway's place and I know the sorts of people he got involved with. Listen. If I can help you, the only way I can do that is if I admit to some bad stuff. Stuff I've put a long way behind me. I don't wanna end up being questioned or charged or anything.'

'What sort of "stuff" are we talking about?' Culverhouse asked, keen not to commit to anything.

'Not as bad as torching a bloke's house and killing him, if that's what you mean.'

Culverhouse sat back in his chair and crossed his arms. 'Listen, if you've got information that you think might help, it'd be a good idea to tell me. If it's information that could change the investigation, and you don't tell me, you could be perverting the course of justice.'

'I know... It just ain't that easy. I'm exposed big time here.'

Culverhouse rolled his eyes again. 'Alright. Let's look at this from another angle. What would you say if this wasn't you sitting here, but a friend of yours? Say that friend had information that could help.'

'He should help,' Tyrone said. 'It'd be the right thing to do.'

'Well there you go, then.'

'But it ain't easy for him, y'know?'

'Yeah, I know. You've told me three times. What do you reckon the bad stuff is that this... mate... of yours might not want to admit to?'

Tyrone shuffled uncomfortable in his seat. 'You wired?'

'No. Pat me down if you like.'

Tyrone thought for a moment, then shook his head. 'Let's say, this friend of mine, maybe, like, he was involved in a gang that did an armed robbery or something.'

'Something like... Oh, let's just pick one at random, shall we? Like Trenton-Lowe, for example?'

Tyrone looked down at his hands. 'Yeah. Like that one.'

Culverhouse nodded. 'Then I'd tell your friend that first of all he's a fucking idiot for inviting a police officer to a meeting to admit to being involved with shooting a police officer in the face. And second of all,' he said, noticing the worried look on Tyrone's face, 'I'd point out that it's a case that closed years ago and that time has been served. Most importantly, by the shooter. Then I'd ask him if people were leaning on him and making it awkward for him to talk.'

'Yeah. You got it in one,' Tyrone replied.

'And I'd ask him if one of those people might have died recently. In a fire, perhaps.'

Tyrone didn't reply, but Culverhouse could see from the look on his face that he was spot on.

'That's not all, though, is it?' Culverhouse asked.

Tyrone clenched his jaw and shut his eyes, before taking a deep breath. 'Fuck's sake, I shouldn't be talking about any of this. It's not something I've ever told anyone. Listen, all these years it's been fine. We had a vow of silence, no-one broke it, no-one got hurt. I kept up my end of the bargain. I never spoke to no-one about nothing. But someone's started threatening me.'

'Someone involved in the Trenton-Lowe job?'

'I dunno. Yeah, I think so. I think it's all connected, but I dunno how. I just get a vibe, y'know? Listen, you know John Lucas got out of prison, right? The day Freddie Galloway's house gets burned down. That ain't right, is it? That weren't him. I can guarantee it.'

'So what are you saying? You know who it was?'

'I think so, yeah. There was only four of us involved.'

Culverhouse tried to work it out in his head. 'You, John Lucas, Freddie Galloway and Benjamin Newell?'

'Yeah. He got sent down for a little while but not as long as Lucas. Lucas totally took the rap 'cos he pulled the trigger. That night, Lucas and Newell left by the front entrance, where we came in. Me and Freddie went out the back. The whole thing was Freddie's idea, he had the inside contact. He put the team together. Me and Freddie got away from there. Never identified, nothing. No-one ever blabbed. But Lucas took the rap, right? So I totally get that he'd want to get even. It makes sense for him to want to torch Freddie Galloway's place and probably to come after me next.'

'But you don't think he did?'

Tyrone shook his head. 'Nah. Doesn't feel right. But Benjamin Newell got fucked over too that night. He got caught while me and Freddie escaped out the back. And the reason he got caught was because Lucas fired that fucking gun. If they'd got out of there earlier, or gone another way or whatever... Well, y'know. They wouldn't have been caught. And even if they were, Newell wouldn't have got the sentence he did if Lucas hadn't shot the cop.'

'So what you're saying is—'

'What I'm saying is John Lucas weren't the only one who could've held a grudge. Newell had three people to get back at. And wouldn't it be perfect if he'd not only managed to get away with popping Freddie off but managed to pin it on Lucas too? Two for the price of one. Worth waiting eleven years for, don't you reckon?'

Culverhouse had to admit that it might well be. It was starting to sound like a solid theory. 'In that case, how's he going to get back at you?' he asked Tyrone.

'Yeah. That's what I'm worried about.'

29

Culverhouse strode back into the incident room with the intention of grabbing a mug of coffee and sitting in his office with his eyes shut for a few minutes. The Freddie Galloway case was tying him in knots, and he and his team would have no way of knowing who was telling the truth and who was bound by a veil of silence imposed on them by career criminals.

He was half tempted to wind the whole investigation down. After all, a major criminal – one they'd never managed to convict – was dead. Justice had been done in its own twisted way.

He didn't even get as far as the coffee machine, though, before Wendy stopped him in his tracks.

'Call from above, I'm afraid.'

Culverhouse rolled his eyes and sighed. Although he was fortunate that the Chief Constable, Charles Hawes, was generally very supportive of him, the boss was always acutely aware of the public perception of the local police force. More than that, he had to maintain a positive image of Mildenheath Police and its CID department to avoid it being subsumed into county headquarters at Milton House — the only town CID department that hadn't been. Having Mildenheath CID moved to Milton House would mean being tied up in the bureaucracy that came with it — something Hawes did his level best to avoid at all times. That was why he'd retained an office at Mildenheath and preferred to base himself there as opposed to county headquarters.

'It's day two. What's he sticking his beak in for already?' Culverhouse asked, not expecting an answer. Regardless, he poured himself a mug of black coffee from the machine and made his way up the stairs to the Chief Constable's office. When he got there, he knocked on the door and waited for Hawes to invite him in.

'Jack.'

'You wanted a word with me, sir.'

'Yes, Jack. Sit down.'

Culverhouse tried not to look annoyed. The Chief Constable had a reputation for lecturing him and thinking that just asking for results would make them happen quicker. Of course, Culverhouse knew that results would happen when they happened, and not because the Chief Constable had asked for them.

'I just wanted to see where we are with the arson and death in Little Walgrave. Are you treating it as murder?'

'We're still looking into it, sir. We don't have a full

awareness of what happened or whether the arsonist deliberately tried to kill the victim.'

'They burnt his house down in the middle of the night, Jack. They knew he'd be tucked up in bed. How can you judge it to be anything but murder?'

Culverhouse desperately wanted to tell the Chief Constable to stop interfering, but he didn't.

'Truth is, Jack, I'd prefer it not to be a murder. All Chief Constables would, I'm sure. Doesn't look good for the county figures.'

Culverhouse knew that wasn't true. Another murder in the Mildenheath area meant there was even more justification for keeping the CID department open, and ensuring he stayed twenty miles away from the office managers and pen pushers at Milton House.

'We're doing our best, sir. We've got a list of suspects and we've already had one in for questioning.'

'So I hear,' the Chief Constable said, leaning back in his chair and steepling his hands. 'John Lucas, wasn't it? The same John Lucas who got out of prison a few hours earlier.' Hawes's voice rose in both volume and intonation. 'It makes a mockery of justice if he's been allowed to do that. I mean, what's the bloody point? We know a large percentage of prisoners go on to reoffend, but what the hell's going on if a man can get out of prison after eleven years and burn someone's bloody house down the same day?'

'I agree, sir,' Culverhouse said. 'But there's not a whole lot we can do about it. It's down to the prison service when someone is released and to keep an eye on their probation.'

'We have a responsibility, Jack. In the public's eyes if nothing else. And how the hell can the prison officers not spot that the guy's still holding a massive grudge? Don't the parole board look for those sorts of things?'

'With respect, sir, we don't know that it is John Lucas. There are other suspects and information pointing to other people.'

'What, better information than finding half the tools at his bloody house?'

Culverhouse had to admit that it didn't look good on that front. The evidence pointing to John Lucas seemed overwhelming – almost too overwhelming. 'To be fair, sir, it's not up to us to babysit John Lucas. The police's job ended years ago when they secured a conviction.'

'That's not the point, Jack. We should have been all over this. Someone should have been.'

'What do you propose then?' Culverhouse replied, trying not to lose his temper. 'Undercover officers watching every scrote who's released from prison? We're stretched to the limit as it is and budgets are being cut even more. We haven't even got enough money to stock the toilets with bog roll. My team's short staffed already, and now DS Knight wants to piss off for the day to do her exams. I'm sorry, sir, but it's just not on. I'm not taking the rap for this one.'

Hawes ignored Culverhouse's anger. 'How is she doing? DS Knight, I mean. With her exam prep.'

'I dunno. Alright, I think.'

'She'd make a good inspector, you know.'

'Yes, I know. That's why I suggested she take the exams in the first place.'

'But now you're not so sure?'

Culverhouse sighed. 'I am sure, yes. But the timing is fucking dreadful, pardon my French. DC Weston's away for the foreseeable future and we were short-staffed enough before that.'

'It's one day, Jack.' Hawes said.

'Plus all the time she'd have to spend revising beforehand. It'd distract from her work here. We can't afford that at the moment.'

Hawes leaned forward and spoke quietly. 'You need to allow her to do it, Jack. For the sake of her career. We'll manage.'

'No. Sorry,' Culverhouse replied, folding his arms. 'I'm not compromising this investigation. Especially seeing as that's the whole reason you invited me here, to tell me we need to do more.'

'We can always do more, Jack. Especially in the eyes of the public. You know that. Would it help to have a meeting with the senior investigating officer who covered the Trenton-Lowe robbery?'

'No, I don't think so,' Culverhouse replied, perhaps a little too quickly. The SIO on that case had been Malcolm Pope, then a Detective Inspector, now a DCI stationed at Milton House, who Culverhouse – and most of the rest of the CID unit – despised. His polished, shiny exterior was just a smokescreen for his very average success rate and revolting personality. The bosses, though, loved him and couldn't see past his golden boy image.

'I thought you might say that. He'll try and get involved, though, you know. He still sees this as his case.'

'Yeah, well he can piss off. He's not coming anywhere near it.'

Hawes nodded slowly. 'Then you know what you need to do, Jack.'

30

After meeting DCI Culverhouse, Tyrone had milled around in town for a bit longer to run some errands. He'd picked up some bits for dinner, bought a new tea towel to replace the yellowing once-white one in the kitchen in the flat and finally had the cracked screen on his mobile phone replaced.

He was still a little shaken after his chat with Culverhouse, so returning to the normal boring routine had helped him to keep calm and forget the threatening note he'd received earlier that day.

He hadn't told Culverhouse about the note. He didn't see how it was relevant, although deep down he knew it all had to be connected somehow. His life up until the last couple of days had been relatively quiet for years. What were the odds of someone finding out about his visits to Lenny within hours of John Lucas getting out of jail and Freddie Galloway being killed? Tyrone was no mathematician, but he didn't fancy those odds. He knew what those sorts of people were like.

The weather was looking good, so he decided that rather than sit on a stuffy bus all the way back home, he'd walk some of the way back and catch another bus further along the way once he'd had enough of walking.

He was about to turn off the main road past the industrial estate and walk up Edgefield Avenue when his phone pinged in his headphones, the sound of a text message coming through, interrupting the new Stormzy album. He took his phone out of his pocket and read the message.

A dirty fuckin poof n a grass! U no wot happens wen u chat 2 law

He didn't recognise the number, but he didn't need to. He had his suspicions. He looked behind him, back towards the main road. Whoever had sent this message knew he had met Jack Culverhouse earlier that day, so there was every chance they could be watching him now. There was no-one behind him, though, so he quickened his pace and decided to take a shortcut across Edgefield Park rather than walking around the footpath outside the perimeter.

As he walked across the grass, he thought he heard a sound behind him. He turned round, but again saw nothing. Again, he quickened his pace, the gate on the far side of the park now in sight.

He estimated he was probably now about fifty metres from the gate, then it was another fifty metres or so down the road until he'd be back on another main road, where there'd be plenty of witnesses and CCTV. Then he'd be almost home and dry.

He knew he shouldn't have come out today. Not while he was feeling like this, like he had to watch over his shoulder at every moment. Ever since Headache had been released from prison, he knew things were going to be different. He knew he was always going to be warier, that things weren't the way they had been for the past few years. There was stability, a sense that things were in the past and were staying there. Until they inevitably all got dragged up again, that was.

Tyrone knew he couldn't change his past. Who could? The best you could hope for was to deal with things in the only way you knew how. Either that or find a better way. Life didn't tend to give you too many options on that front.

But stability had helped. Every day had been a day further away from those days, although it had always been at the back of his mind that it was also a day closer to the inevitable – to the day he knew the past would come back to haunt them all.

He'd been weighing up his options and quickly realised he didn't have any. He didn't have the money to move away and start somewhere new. And, in any case, why should he have to? He had no right to feel guilty about anything, to feel victimised. Even if he had, starting afresh somewhere else wouldn't be as straightforward as it sounded. Where would he go? How would he start to lay down new roots? A black guy from a council estate couldn't just fit right in on a strange council estate miles from home, and perhaps less so in a quiet country village somewhere. The way the world was, the way society operated, he was stuck exactly where God had dumped him the day he was born. Social mobility didn't exist when you were one of the people society kept immobile.

As he went to walk around the outside of the empty kids' playground and onto the path towards the exit from Edgefield Park, he became suddenly aware of a presence behind him – almost right on top of him, making him wonder how the hell he hadn't spotted anyone.

He didn't have time to think, though. He barely had time to put his hands out in front of him as he went crashing to the ground, a skull-splitting pain shooting through him as he tasted blood and tried not to choke on it, instinctively bringing his arms up to cover his head as the black boot swung towards him.

He felt the crunch of his nasal cartilage and the sensation of warm blood pouring down over his mouth as he curled tightly into a ball, his head ringing and orientation screwed, knowing he could do very little at this stage other than pray to God the beating ended soon.

31

The rest of the team had noticed Jack Culverhouse's demeanour as he came back from his meeting with the Chief Constable, and they all knew it would be best to give him a wide berth for the rest of the day. He wasn't a man who hid his thoughts or feelings particularly well — not when it came to work, anyway — and the team knew the tell-tale signs that meant you were likely to get your head bitten off if you tried to talk to him.

Steve Wing, though, didn't have much choice. The call he'd just taken on his phone could potentially have an impact on the investigation into Freddie Galloway's death, and keeping it from Culverhouse would only make him angrier when he eventually discovered what it was. Steve told the rest of the team what he'd discovered, and they all agreed that it could be very significant.

Holding his breath, he paused and knocked on the door of Culverhouse's office.

'What?' came the barked response from the other side of the door. Steve took this as an invitation to enter.

'Sorry to disturb you,' he said, 'but I've just taken a call which might have a bearing on Operation Mandible.'

'Go on.'

'Benjamin Newell, the shit safecracker on the Trenton-Lowe job. He got married at the weekend.'

'That's lovely, Steve. Send him a card from me.'

'I wouldn't bother if I were you,' Steve replied. 'Looks like it might be one of the shortest marriages in history. He decked one of his new wife's work colleagues at the evening do.'

Culverhouse looked up at Steve for the first time since the DS had walked into the office. 'Oh, did he now? The nice, newly reformed, born again Christian Benjamin Newell, you mean?'

Steve raised his eyebrows. 'That's the one. His new wife's gone off to stay with her parents. No arrests made, but word got back to us via an officer's sister, who was at the do.'

'Well, that sounds to me like the hallmark of a man who reacts very badly when provoked or when he holds a grudge against someone, wouldn't you say?'

'I'd say it's worth having a word with him, yeah.'

'Who went out to speak to him after Galloway was found dead?' Culverhouse asked.

The other officers looked at each other, before soon realising that no-one was speaking up.

'Are you taking the piss?' the DCI said, his voice rising.

'This bloke's done time because of Galloway's job that went wrong, and no-one thought to go and speak to him about the fact Galloway's just been killed?'

Frank Vine spoke up quietly from the back of the room. 'It wasn't given as an action in any briefings, guv.'

Culverhouse fired his trademark icy glare at Frank. 'Do you need me to give you an action to wipe your arse? No. I didn't think I needed to state the bleedin' obvious to you.' He looked around the room, before mumbling, 'Want a job doing, do it your bloody self,' and grabbing his coat. 'Knight,' he said, raising his voice again. 'Get your arse over here. You're coming with me.'

32

John Lucas entered the local branch of Pemberry's and watched as the man behind the counter finished cutting a new set of keys. A young woman was resoling a pair of black shoes a few feet away from him.

The man registered Lucas's arrival and greeted him.

'Good afternoon. Can I help you?'

Lucas shuffled awkwardly. 'Uh, yes, I'm looking for John Ayling.'

'Ah,' the man said, a look of faint recognition crossing his face. 'You must be John Lucas.'

Lucas nodded.

'Come with me,' the man said. 'Lucy, can you hold the fort for a few minutes?'

The girl nodded, and Lucas followed the shop's manager behind the counter and out into the office at the rear.

Ayling closed the door behind them. 'So. I got the message from your probation officer yesterday.'

Lucas recognised what Ayling was doing. He was leaving it open, giving him the chance to explain himself in his own words. The problem was, he knew Ayling had probably made his mind up already.

'I don't know what to say,' Lucas replied. 'Something happened with one of the people I used to be involved with, and the police took me in to speak to me.'

'Arrested you, I heard.'

'Yeah.'

'What for?'

Lucas took a deep breath. 'Arson and manslaughter.'

Ayling raised his eyebrows and scratched the back of his head. 'And have they bailed you or released you?'

'Bailed me. There was... There was stuff in my garage which they reckon linked me to what happened. But it's all bollocks. I've not even been in that garage since I got out of prison. They'll do forensics or fingerprints or something and they'll find out it wasn't me. But in the meantime I've got this all hanging over me.'

'You sound pretty sure they'll drop it. I've got to say, John, your probation officer didn't sound quite so certain.'

'Yeah, well the probation officer isn't me, is she? I'm me, and I know I didn't do it.'

'Alright. Fine. But how do we know? I'm not going to lie to you, John, we get a lot of ex-offenders working for Pemberry's. It's one of the things we do, trying to help them integrate back into the community and give them a second chance. That's a big thing to do. Not many other retailers or businesses would be willing to take that chance. But we need something in return. We can't just take on everyone who comes out of prison regardless of who they are or what they do. We have a zero tolerance approach when it comes to reoffending.'

'But I haven't reoffended!'

'No, but you have been arrested for an offence within hours of being released. I appreciate the police are investigating and that they'll decide to either charge you or release you — hopefully the latter — but in the meantime there's very little we can do. The same rules apply to all our staff, whether they're ex-offenders or not. If you're under investigation for a potentially serious crime, we have to suspend you from work.'

Lucas closed his eyes. He feared that would be the case. And all before he'd even come into the shop and done his first day's work.

'We're not trying to make a judgement, but we have certain responsibilities as a retailer and an employer,' Ayling said. 'I hope you understand.'

'So what, I'm out before I'm even in?'

'No, it's a temporary suspension. Just while this is all up in the air. You've got to look at it from our point of view, John. You haven't even started working here yet. We've never met you before. And the first thing we hear is that you're not turning up for your first day of work because you've been arrested. For arson and manslaughter.'

'Yeah, and then bailed a few hours later. They don't

just bail people on an arson and manslaughter case, especially not if they're ex-cons. The only reason they'd do that is if they didn't really believe I'd done it.'

'In which case they'll drop the case and release you fully in due course, at which point you'll be more than welcome to come back and join us here.'

'And if they don't?'

'Like you say, you didn't do it. So that's not an option, is it?'

Lucas tried to hold his frustrations inside, but he was struggling. He desperately wanted to tell Ayling to stuff his stupid job. He could stick it up his arse as far as he cared. But he knew that wouldn't do him any favours.

He wanted the job. It wasn't exactly a burgeoning career, but what else would he have in his position? He was fortunate to have that much. He just prayed to God – if there was one – that whoever had tried setting him up hadn't done it too well.

Then again, they'd had eleven years to plan it. What if they'd covered every angle, thought of every possible way in which their plan might fall down?

He knew he was innocent. But he didn't have the same level of trust in the British justice system as most people did. And he knew what some of his past associates were capable of.

He had to hope, had to pray that logic and common sense would win out. Because he already had too much to lose if it didn't.

33

As Benjamin Newell hadn't been arrested for the assault on Ollie Hardcastle, Wendy Knight and Jack Culverhouse went to visit him at his home. This was the sort of man who'd likely give you more in an informal statement than he would in an official interview situation.

Newell's home certainly had traces of a female influence, although it looked as though that influence had been absent for the past couple of days.

'Missus not in?' Culverhouse said, after the introductions had been made and Newell had ushered them through into the living room.

'Uh, no,' he said, scratching the back of his head. 'She's not.'

'Not nipped out to the shops for a pint of milk, I'm guessing.'

'No. She's staying with her parents.'

'Interesting choice of honeymoon.'

'Yeah, well it's cheaper than the Seychelles,' Newell said, sitting down in an armchair.

'How long's she away for?' Wendy asked, sitting down on the sofa next to Culverhouse.

Benjamin Newell shook his head. 'No idea. You tell me. How long do women need to get their heads straight?'

Wendy wanted to say she didn't know because she didn't tend to go for men who started fights on their own wedding day, but decided against it. She hadn't had the best track record when it came to dating, but she could honestly say she'd so far managed to avoid the violent types. Maybe it was her background as a police officer. Perhaps she could spot them a mile off, or them her.

'So, what happened?' she asked.

Newell looked at them for a moment before averting his eyes back towards the carpet. 'I'm guessing you already know that. This isn't a social call, I take it.'

'We do need it in your own words,' Culverhouse said.

Newell looked at them again. 'Aren't you arresting me?'

'We just want to get your version of events at the moment,' Wendy replied.

Newell's eyes narrowed. 'Nah, this is something else, isn't it? If that Hardcastle prick had made a complaint or pressed charges, you'd have arrested me on the doorstep and asked questions later. So if this isn't about the incident at the wedding, what is it?'

Wendy looked at Culverhouse, whose face told her she should try to stick to the agreed line of conversation for now.

'It's to do with an incident we think might be connected in some way. We haven't arrested you because we're not accusing you of anything. We just want to get some background information that might help us with our enquiries.'

'What enquiries? Something Hardcastle's done? If it is, count me in. I'd love to see that little wanker get sent down.'

'Does the name Frederick Galloway mean anything to you?' Culverhouse asked, going straight for the jugular. Occasionally, it was necessary to jerk an interviewee with a short, sharp shock, then watch their reaction as they were jolted into reality. He could see from Benjamin Newell's face that it'd had the desired effect.

'You know damn well it does,' Newell replied after a few seconds. 'You didn't come out here without looking at my record first.'

'Freddie Galloway died in an arson attack on his home the other night,' Culverhouse said.

Benjamin Newell swallowed, but otherwise gave no reaction.

'You don't seem too surprised to hear that,' Wendy said.

'Yeah, well, news travels fast round these parts.'

'Good news or bad news?' Culverhouse asked.

'Both,' came the response.

'So you're not upset to hear that your old boss died slowly and painfully in his own home?'

'He wasn't my boss.'

'He ran the Trenton-Lowe job. The one you did three and a half years' porridge for.'

'Yeah, well I wasn't the only one.'

Culverhouse nodded slowly. 'I know. There were two of you who had good reason to hold a grudge against Freddie Galloway.'

He left this hanging in the air for a few moments, watching as Benjamin Newell tried to formulate his next response.

'I don't do grudges,' he said, eventually.

'And what about John Lucas?' Wendy asked.

'What about him?'

'Does he hold grudges?'

'You'd have to ask him that, wouldn't you?' Newell folded his arms and leaned back in the chair.

'Are you aware that John Lucas has been released from prison?' Wendy asked.

Benjamin Newell seemed to start blinking faster than usual. 'I heard someone mention something, yeah.'

'He was released on the same day Freddie Galloway's house burnt down,' Culverhouse said. 'A few hours earlier, in fact.'

Newell was silent for a few moments, before raising his shoulders and upturned palms like a caricature French waiter. 'And what do you want me to do about that?'

'Well, offer us your thoughts and opinions, perhaps,' Culverhouse replied. 'Did John Lucas hold a grudge against Freddie Galloway? Enough to want to burn his house down and kill him a few hours after getting out of prison, knowing damn well the trail would lead straight to him?' He could see from Newell's face that he didn't agree with this line of thinking. 'What is it? You know something, don't you?'

Newell shook his head. 'No. I don't know nothing. All I do know is John Lucas weren't stupid. Listen, he'd been inside a long time. He had a lot of space to think and plan something if he was going to do it. He wouldn't just come out, go round and torch the place. That'd be stupid.'

Culverhouse had to agree. But that left only one or two possibilities. Either John Lucas *was* that stupid, or someone else had set him up. The only person they could find who had a direct grudge against Galloway and was connected to Lucas was Newell himself, so why would he all but acquit Lucas, knowing suspicion would fall on himself as a result? Something still didn't feel right.

'Do you have a habit of reacting quickly and violently, Mr Newell?' Culverhouse asked, again trying to catch him off guard.

'How do you mean?'

'I mean, for example, reacting to another man talking flirtatiously about your wife by kicking his head in at your own wedding, or perhaps reacting to one of your old criminal accomplices being released from prison by burning someone's house down to try and frame him.'

'You still haven't arrested me, Detective Chief Inspector,' Newell said, avoiding the question.

'I'm well aware of that,' Culverhouse replied. 'But let's face it. John Lucas was the reason you went down, wasn't he?'

'I went down because I got caught by a traffic patrol car driving away from the scene.'

'Yes, and you would've had a fine and a slap on the

wrist for driving without insurance, if it hadn't been for John Lucas blasting half a pound of lead shot into a policeman's face.'

Culverhouse could see Newell's jaw moving as he ground his teeth.

'I served my time. So did John. He served three times what I did, too. Justice was done. I'm happy with that. I've changed now. I'm a family man.'

'A family man who hides a dark secret, Mr Newell. A family man who can't even keep that darkness under wraps on his own wedding day.'

'Listen, you would've reacted in exactly the same way if someone had said that about your missus,' Newell said, looking at Culverhouse.

'Would I?' the DCI replied, his voice level, locking eyes with Newell.

'Yes. Yes, you would. Now, are you going to arrest me or not?'

'That depends,' Wendy said, trying to defuse the situation. 'Where were you on the night Freddie Galloway died?'

'In the evening I was out for a few drinks with some mates. It was the night before my wedding. Then I stayed at my mate Cameron's place to get ready the next morning.'

'And they can vouch for that?' Wendy asked.

'Yeah. So can a pub-full of people and the taxi driver who picked us up the next morning.'

Wendy knew the next step would be to check the mobile phone triangulation from Benjamin Newell's phone, which would tell them exactly where he – or, at least, his phone – had been during those hours. It wouldn't categorically prove his innocence, but if he was lying and took his phone with him to Freddie Galloway's house, it'd be pretty damning evidence in court.

Wendy smiled and nodded. 'Thank you for your time, Mr Newell. We'll be in touch.'

As they got back in the car outside, Culverhouse let out a huge sigh. 'We'll need to get a trace put on his phone. See who he calls now.'

'Already done,' Wendy replied, fastening her seatbelt. 'If he panics and calls someone, we'll know about it straight away. That should've been enough to put him into panic mode if he was involved.'

'And if he wasn't?'

Wendy took her turn to sigh. 'Then we've got a lot of work on our plate.'

34

Jack sat in his dark office, having sent the rest of the team home for the night. There wasn't anything they could realistically do at this stage, and if any news were to come about overnight the call handlers would ring him. Amongst Mildenheath CID's many interesting quirks was that shift work just didn't happen. The unit was too small to accommodate it, so it was more often than not a case of working whatever hours were required, whenever possible.

He liked to sit in the dark solitude of his office once everyone had gone home. It gave him time to think, relax and reflect. If he went straight home he'd have his daughter, Emily, around the place. It wasn't that he didn't like her being there – on the contrary, he loved it – but sometimes he needed time and space to himself.

He flicked absentmindedly through his phone, the bright colours of the dating app's icon catching his eye. He hovered his finger over the icon, remembering how Mackenzie and the others had talked him into setting up a profile, and how stupid an idea he'd thought it. He could just hold his finger down, click the X and delete it there and then.

But something was telling him otherwise. Surely a quick look wouldn't hurt, right? He opened the app, and noticed a red dot over the Messages icon, indicating that he had new, unread messages waiting for him. He tapped his finger on it and found the message. It was from a woman called Christine K. The app demanded its users go under their real names, but hid their surnames behind an initial.

Christine K: Hey you! Why the secrecy? I'm intrigued... X

It took him a moment to realise what she was going on about. Although the app stipulated that users should only upload real photos of themselves, Jack had used an obscure close-up picture of one of his eyes. He didn't know why he'd chosen that particular shot, but he didn't really want to be recognised on there, so had immediately changed it from the photo Ryan had taken of him.

Slowly, he tapped out a reply.

Because I'm an international man of mystery. Can't have the Russians spotting me on here. My cover would be blown.

He hit *Send*. Within seconds, three dots were dancing

across the screen, indicating that Christine was typing a reply. He took the time to tap on her profile picture to get a closer look. He vaguely remembered seeing her on the app when Ryan set it up, and presumably must have indicated his approval by tapping the green tick rather than the red cross. He scrolled through her photos, and liked what he saw. Sure, perhaps she was a dress size above the sort of women he usually went for, but at his age he couldn't afford to be too picky. In any case, Claudia Schiffer was hardly likely to be hanging around on dating apps.

A new message popped up at the top of his screen, so he navigated back to the Messages section to read it.

Christine K: Sounds like fun! Do you get to carry a gun? X

The problem with sending messages online was that tone of voice was lost. He assumed she couldn't be stupid enough to have actually believed his message, so typed out his reply in the same vein of humour.

I don't need to. I can kill a horse with my bare hands.

He waited to see her response. She was either going to like his sense of humour or be put off by it. He'd got used to that over the years.

Christine K: Now why would you want to do that? X

No choice. Restaurants round here are terrible.

He looked out of his window across the rooftops in Mildenheath town centre. It wasn't the prettiest sight in the world, but it was all he had. The town needed cleaning up in more ways than one. Despite the multitude of regeneration plans the council had put forward over the years, nothing seemed to ever be happening on that front. In the meantime, the buildings got older and more dilapidated, and the once-pretty market town had begun to look more tired than ever.

He'd lost count of the number of memories he had of this place. They weren't even divided into good or bad. They were just memories. Cases, incidents, drama. Mildenheath was a town that seemed to thrive on drama. If truth be told, many of the residents didn't have anything better to do. He always felt sorry for the first response teams in uniform, being constantly called out to domestic disputes, arguments over Facebook and people who just didn't know how to get along with others. And then, of course, there was the occasional but increasingly frequent dead body. Underneath the pathetic and laughable exterior of many parts of the town, there was a dark underbelly which — fortunately — few residents ever had to encounter. There were times when he felt jealous of his colleagues in uniform dealing with innocent Facebook brawls.

His phone vibrated again, and he looked at the screen.

Christine K: Why don't you show me? X

His mind was elsewhere and he had no idea what she was talking about.

What do you mean?

Christine K: The local restaurants. Pick a really dreadful one and take me along to show me how bad it is. At least the local horses will sleep soundly x

Jack looked at this message for a few moments. It was a long time since a woman had asked him out. It had been almost as long since he'd looked at a woman with anything other than superficial appreciation. Was this even an offer of a date or was he reading too much into it? He was out of practise, that was for sure.

A date?

Jack wasn't sure which response he wanted to see appear next. He went back to her profile and looked at her pictures again. Yes, she was definitely attractive. She seemed friendly, bubbly and confident, too, from what little interaction they'd had over a mobile private messaging system.

His phone vibrated with another reply.

Yes, a date. You game? X

He read the words again, twice, then swallowed hard,

locked his phone and put it back in his pocket. He leaned back in his chair and closed his eyes.

35

The first cup of coffee in the morning was always the most valuable. It was like liquid gold to Jack. He didn't care how hot it was, either. Once it was in the cup and the bitter aroma was assaulting his nostrils, there was no stopping him.

Having taken a good healthy slug, he unlocked his mobile phone and fired off a text to his daughter.

Sorry. Will explain later x

He thought she probably wouldn't be awake yet, but the response was almost instantaneous.

Honestly, don't worry. I'm used to it x

That response almost broke his heart. He knew what she meant, though. She wasn't just used to having her father come home at a different time every day — if at all — but was used to fending for herself. Even her mother had abandoned her after taking her away from Jack, and he doubted whether his ex-wife's parents had been much better guardians to her. It was extraordinary that she'd turned out to be as level-headed as she was. That was one of the many complicated reasons why he gave her so much slack.

He thought about replying to her, telling her he'd make it up to her, but he knew that was a promise he couldn't be certain to keep. In this job, there were no certainties at all.

'Morning,' came the familiar voice of Wendy Knight as she strolled into the incident room. 'Christ. You look like you've been here all night.'

'Piss off,' Culverhouse grunted.

'Ah. First coffee,' she said, pointing at the mug. 'I'll give you a few minutes to catch up with the rest of mankind. Let me know when the brain's switched on.'

Sometimes, Culverhouse wondered who was the superior officer. The small, tight-knit team had a dynamic like no other. It was almost as if the traditional roles of Detective Chief Inspector, Detective Sergeant and Detective Constable didn't exist. When the shit hit the fan and someone had to take the rap, though, he knew he would very definitely be the head of the unit and the person ultimately responsible.

Wendy would make a good inspector, there was no doubt about that. She seemed to have a way of knowing how to manage people, how to get the best out of them.

When he'd become DCI there was none of this performance management bullshit around. He was just the Detective Sergeant who'd been on the team longest and wanted the job. He'd had a chat with his superiors, done an exam and got his stripes. True enough, he'd been earmarked as the next DCI for a little while before then, while the unit was under the tutelage of Robin Grundy. In those days, a nod from the incumbent DCI was enough to more or less guarantee you the job, pending paperwork.

People often said that Jack Culverhouse was resistant to the changing world of policing, but he knew that was bullshit. The world of policing had already changed, long ago. The line had long been crossed. He wasn't resisting anything; he was just carrying on the same way he always had done. The way that got results. And in a town like Mildenheath, that was all that mattered.

He wondered whether Wendy Knight would get the same sort of results if and when she became a Senior Investigating Officer. A few years ago, he would've said no. But he was starting to see a different side to her, a side that told him that perhaps she wasn't completely closed off to a few of the old-school ideas. She was still one hell of a long way from being Jack Culverhouse's protégé, but she certainly wasn't the goody-two-shoes Detective Sergeant who'd first tiptoed into his office on that first investigation into the suspicious death of Ella Barrington, which ended up becoming a manhunt for a serial killer – a manhunt that was to have devastating and long-lasting personal consequences for Wendy.

He admired her resilience during and after that case. The effects had been clear, but she rarely let it impact on her work. He couldn't say the same about his own personal life, and for that he had to give her credit where credit was due.

'What's your secret, then?' he called over to her. 'You don't look like someone who's been up all night swotting up from Blackstone's.'

'That's because I haven't,' Wendy said, her voice subdued. 'Not much point if I'm going to have to wait until next year to take the exams. Might as well get this case out of the way first, then look at my options.'

Culverhouse walked over to her. 'What do you mean, options? You thinking about not bothering at all?'

Wendy sighed. 'I don't know. I'll think about it more next year. I've got other things on my mind at the moment.'

He looked at Wendy as she absentmindedly shuffled through a pile of papers on her desk, noticing that she looked utterly dejected when the subject of her inspector's exams had been brought up. He couldn't help but feel responsible for that.

Everywhere around him recently, he'd seen people trying but failing. Local people living on council estates, trying to get by in life without a chance in the world. His own colleagues, trying to combine a personal life with their careers and failing miserably. Even last night, the invitation from Christine asking him out on a date. He hadn't even bothered to reply to the poor woman. And what had she done to deserve that? He told himself he'd reply to her later today, and apologise for not getting back to her sooner. If truth be told, though, he was worried. Could he start dating again at his age? He had to be honest and say he had no real interest in it, but the thought did intrigue him. Could he really be happy after all?

'Listen, I've... uh... been having a few thoughts on that, actually,' he said. 'And I think you should go for it.'

'But what about the case?' Wendy asked.

Jack shrugged his shoulders. 'Sod the case. We're not getting anywhere as it is, and this time it's not down to a lack of resources for once. No-one connected with Freddie Galloway is willing to talk, and having an extra person sitting behind a desk isn't going to change that.'

'I won't need to take time off. I'll just need a bit of leeway in not working past my allotted hours.'

'Yeah, well, I'm sure we can sort something out.'

'Are you sure?' Wendy asked. 'You seemed to be totally against the idea last time we spoke, what with Debbie having to take time off and—'

'Look, just shut up and get on with it before I change my mind, alright?'

Wendy smiled, and before she knew what she was doing she'd embraced her DCI in a hug.

'Thank you,' she said. 'Seriously. Thank you.'

36

Tyrone couldn't remember a time he'd been in so much pain. At least in the boxing ring the referee would call a halt to proceedings if you were getting your arse handed to you on a plate. When you got beaten up in the street – or a park – though, things were very different.

The boxing ring allowed you to see your opponent, too. You knew what was happening and could prepare. When someone jumps you from behind, a boxer has about as much chance of fighting back as anyone else. That was something Tyrone was acutely aware of as he lay in his hospital bed, his head throbbing, his ribs in agony every time he took a breath.

'How are you feeling, Tyrone?' the nurse asked him, as she adjusted the drip that was hanging up next to his bed.

'Great,' he mumbled, the effort hurting his ribs.

'The police are here. They want to talk to you about what happened. Are you up to that?'

He sorely wanted to say no, wanted the nurse to tell them to piss off. But he knew they'd only be back later. At least this way he could use his present condition to end the conversation early if he wanted to.

He made a face and gesture that told the nurse he wasn't particularly bothered either way. She smiled and left the room.

A minute or two later, he saw a man he recognised as DCI Culverhouse come onto the ward, accompanied by a younger woman he hadn't seen before.

'We meet again, Tyrone,' Culverhouse said.

'What they sent you for?' Tyrone croaked.

'Ah. You were expecting a wet-behind-the-ears uniformed constable, weren't you? Didn't expect CID to come in to take a witness statement. Thing is, we're not daft. It's our job to find links and make connections. So when you mentioned Trenton-Lowe, we did a bit of digging. And what do you know? A couple of hours later you're duffed up in the park and brought in here. Just another massive coincidence, of course. Anyone connected with the Trenton-Lowe job seems to be plagued by them. Only thing is, I don't believe in coincidences,' Culverhouse said, sitting down on the chair next to Tyrone's bed. 'I believe in joining the dots. And you're going to help me. This is Detective Sergeant Knight, by the way. She can write really quickly, so feel free to start whenever you're ready.'

Tyrone glanced at Wendy, then looked up at the polystyrene-tiled ceiling and closed his eyes.

'I got jumped. I dunno who it was or why they did it. It's a rough area. It happens.'

Culverhouse shook his head. 'Nah. Remember what I said about coincidences? Besides, people like you don't get jumped. Look at you. You're built like a brick shithouse.'

'Kids,' Tyrone said. 'It's a badge of honour if they manage it. That's why pro boxers get started on in clubs and stuff.'

'Kids? Thought there was only one of them?'

'Kid then.'

Culverhouse snorted. 'So you expect me to believe that a lifelong boxer with a physique like yours can end up like this because he got decked by a scrawny little kid off a local estate?'

'He took me by surprise. It happens.'

'Nah. It doesn't. You know that as well as I do. If it was a kid, you'd have been able to defend yourself. Your whole job, your whole way of life is about defending yourself.'

'He was too quick. He got me on the back of the head before I saw him.'

'Alright,' Culverhouse said, leaning back and crossing his arms. 'So why was nothing taken? You've got the latest iPhone, a decent pair of headphones which I happen to know cost upwards of a hundred quid – joys of having a teenage daughter – and your wallet was still in your pocket. Why'd they not take any of that?'

It was the first time this had crossed Tyrone's mind. He'd been in so much pain and had only recently properly regained consciousness, he hadn't even thought about his phone or his wallet. 'I dunno,' he said.

'I do. Because this wasn't about robbing you, and it wasn't about pride or badges of honour. It was about doing you over because someone very specifically and very deliberately wanted to do you over. So who was it?'

Tyrone grunted. 'I don't know. I told you. I didn't see him.'

Culverhouse stayed silent for a few moments. 'Why were you so afraid when you came to see me yesterday afternoon, Tyrone?'

'I wasn't.'

'Yes you were, you were shitting your pants. I've interviewed enough scrotes over the years to know a pant-shitter when I see one. Who's been on your back, Tyrone? Who's been threatening you?'

'No-one.'

Culverhouse nodded slowly. He reached inside his jacket pocket, took out a mobile phone and dropped it on Tyrone's chest, watching as the man doubled over and yelped in agony.

'Forgot to say, we brought this back for you,' Culverhouse said. 'Standard practice to have a little flick through if a crime's been committed. Like assault, say. We occasionally find the odd clue or two. By the way, you really should change your PIN number. The person's year of birth's always the first thing we try.'

Tyrone looked down at the phone, knowing damn well what was coming next. If they'd got into his phone, they would have read his messages, checked his call logs. He knew it would be easier for him if he told them everything. At least, everything about the text messages and what they meant with the homophobic slurs.

He sighed, closed his eyes and swallowed.

37

'Gay?' Steve Wing asked, his voice showing signs of both shock and disgust in almost equal measure.

'Apparently so,' Culverhouse replied, perched on the edge of a desk. 'He doesn't know who sent the messages, but that's what they're referring to.'

'I still don't get what that's got to do with the Trenton-Lowe thing, or with Freddie Galloway's death, though,' Ryan said, as she cleaned her glasses.

'Well I don't think we're likely to get a confession from the lad in writing unless it involves immunity from prosecution, but between you and me and every other fucker who's listening, Tyrone Golds was one of the people involved with the Trenton-Lowe job. And he's a boxer.'

'Bruno!' Steve Wing yelled out.

'Got it in one. So another suspect for Operation Mandible, right? Wrong. He's got an alibi, and somehow I doubt very much that he's lying about it. He was with a rent boy he uses regularly. Guy by the name of Lenny Harvey.'

'I still don't get it, though,' Frank Vine said. 'Why would he tell you all that? We didn't know he was one of the Trenton-Lowe boys. No-one's worked that out in the last eleven years, so why turn up out of the blue and tell us, just to point out he's got an alibi? He would never have been a suspect.'

'Because he thinks he was being blackmailed,' Wendy said. 'He thinks whoever did kill Freddie Galloway is someone he knows. Someone involved with the gang somewhere along the line. And this guy is making sure Tyrone keeps his mouth shut.'

'But Tyrone doesn't know who it is. So what good's that going to do? All it's done is get us involved, which is the last thing he'd want, surely?'

'You'd think so,' Culverhouse said. 'But I've got a feeling it's a lot more complicated than that. Let's break it down. Let's assume for argument's sake it's John Lucas who started the fire. Let's pretend for a moment he actually is fucking stupid enough to leave his boots and accelerant in his own bloody garage. Why would he then go to the effort of setting up some elaborate blackmail scheme against Tyrone Golds? So what if Tyrone suspected him? It's not Tyrone's suspicions he had to be worried about with that amount of evidence knocking around in his house. It doesn't make sense to me that he'd focus his efforts there. If it was John Lucas, there was no planning or forethought whatsoever. It'd be a half-bottle of scotch and a spark of fury at best.'

'What if it was Tyrone?' Ryan asked. 'What if he set John Lucas up to look like the killer, and set up this whole blackmail thing to strengthen his case?'

'Like I said, he would never have been a suspect. He didn't need to put his head above the parapet. It would've been pointless,' Culverhouse said.

'Not pointless at all, sir. Look at your response there. That's exactly what I mean. What if it was the ultimate double bluff? After all, why the hell would we suspect him if he'd come to us with that? It'd just strengthen suspicion against John Lucas or the others.'

'I dunno. He's got too much to lose by coming out with that. I don't imagine admitting to being gay on that estate is a particularly great idea.'

'Homophobia comes in all shapes and sizes,' Ryan said. 'Trust me.'

'Tyrone had no motive for wanting Galloway dead, either. He and Galloway both got off scot free. It was the other two who went down. He's least likely to have a motive out of the lot of them. So let's say for argument's sake it's our other suspect, Benjamin Newell. He's got form for reacting violently when he hears something he doesn't like. And we now know that Tyrone Golds got in contact with Newell on the night of his wedding, the day after Freddie Galloway's house was burnt down. They arranged to meet at the foot of Mildenheath Common. And before you ask why he'd admit that if it was innocent,' Culverhouse said, looking at Ryan, 'he didn't have much choice. We had his phone records.'

'What was said at the meeting?' Steve asked.

'Well, we've only got Tyrone's word for that at the moment. But he says he was sounding Newell out. Trying to see how he reacted when the subject was brought up. Tyrone's instinct was that Newell was hiding something. It might just be that he was shocked by the news, or that his mind was on what'd just happened at his wedding reception. But either way, Tyrone suspects Newell.'

'He's got an alibi, though,' Wendy said. 'He was in a pub in town the night before, celebrating his last night of freedom. Then he went back to his best man's house, where he stayed the night. His phone's cell trace seems to back that up, but of course there's no guarantee he took his phone with him. If he went, that is.'

'Well someone bloody went,' Culverhouse barked. 'And that means someone's lying to us, if not more than one person.'

'What, you reckon they're all in on it?' Frank asked.

'Wouldn't surprise me. But they're either dumb fucks bringing Tyrone into the mix or they're playing an absolute fucking blinder, running rings around us. Either way, we've got to probe a lot deeper and a lot harder, and not in the way that'd give Tyrone Golds a boner. No offence,' he added, looking at Ryan.

'What about charging John Lucas?' Wendy said. 'That'd give us a lot more time to interview him under caution, and we'd be able to investigate a lot further.'

'Dependant on the CPS. Might be worth putting in for a charge, see what they say.'

'And in the meantime?'

Culverhouse sighed. 'In the meantime, we need to rip up everything we know – or thought we knew – and chuck it in the bin. We need to go straight back to square one.'

38

Culverhouse's head was starting to buzz, either through exhaustion, stress or a caffeine overdose. He hoped it wasn't the latter, though, as he poured himself another mug of black coffee.

'Going to be a long day,' Ryan said, as she sidled up next to him and made herself a cup of tea.

'Mmmmm,' came the response.

'Any matches yet?'

Culverhouse looked at her, waiting for her to elaborate.

'On the app.'

'Don't know what you're talking about.'

'Yes you do. I can tell. And I can tell something's happened with it, too.'

'Isn't there some filing you can be getting on with?'

'It's my job to know when people are hiding something from me. Come on, out with it.

'If it'll bloody shut you up, I got a message from some woman yesterday.'

'What did she say?' Ryan asked.

Culverhouse took his phone out of his pocket, opened the app and plonked the phone down on the sideboard. Ryan picked it up and scrolled through the messages.

'Hey there, Casanova. You've got the hang of this, haven't you? Why didn't you reply, though?'

Culverhouse shrugged. 'Didn't know what to say.'

'Did you think about "yes"?'

'Thought about it,' he replied, shuffling his feet.

'Then say it. You do know she can see that you've read her message, right? It says 8.16pm. All she can see is that you read the message straight away, then didn't bother replying.'

'How?'

Ryan held the phone towards him. 'Look. The little indicator there. If it's just an outline of a heart, it means the message has been sent. If it's filled in red, it means it's been read. She can see you read her message, and as soon as she asked for a date you just bombed out and ignored her.'

Culverhouse had to admit he really didn't understand technology, nor did he like it particularly when it had a habit of spying on him like this.

'So what now?' he asked.

'Now you reply to her as quickly as possible and apologise for not doing it yesterday. Say something came up at work while you were replying and you got sidetracked. Make up some excuse. But whatever you do, say yes. Don't leave her thinking you were just trying to come up with a way to blow her off.'

Culverhouse stood and stared at the phone.

'You do want to meet her, don't you?' Ryan asked.

Culverhouse let out a long lungful of breath. 'I dunno. I mean, yeah, I think so. It's hard to explain, though. It's... It's been a long time.'

'I know. I get that.'

'No you don't, you're twelve.'

'If you say so. But I know what it's like to be out of the game. Mandy was my first proper girlfriend. Not only did I have no real experience of dating before her, but I didn't even know who or what I wanted until then. All I knew is I wasn't particularly interested in boys, and that my love life had been completely non-existent until then. That happens for a lot of people. Sometimes, if you don't know what it is you want, you just assume you want nothing. Until someone comes along and surprises you, and then you realise that was what you wanted all along.'

'I'm not about to turn gay if that's what you mean.'

Ryan laughed. 'No, I guessed that. What I meant was you should meet up with her. See how you get on. You might be surprised. And if you don't like each other, so what? You've lost nothing. But at least this way you know the answer. If you don't meet with her and find out for yourself, you'll never know.'

'Yeah. That's what I'm worried about.'

'What, not knowing?'

'No, turning up and finding out she's some sort of fruit

loop, or worse that she's perfect but doesn't like me. I'm too old to be getting into all that shit again. I've been there, done it, got the t-shirt. And it doesn't fit any more.'

'Fashion changes. Some women like tight. I was talking about the t-shirt, by the way. Listen, just reply to her. Suggest meeting up somewhere for a few drinks and a chat. It'll be better than forever wondering what could have happened.'

'Listen to you,' Culverhouse replied. 'It's some bird who's sent me three messages on a dating app. We're hardly Bonnie and Clyde.'

'No, but you like her and you want to meet her. I can tell. You want to find out more. You're just scared of finding out more because you've been close to women before and you've been burned. There's a large part of you that thinks if you keep yourself to yourself and stay out of the dating scene, you can't get burned again. And you think that a lifetime of solitude and loneliness is better than risking being hurt again, even if that does come at the expense of your own happiness.'

'You sound like a bloody horoscope.'

'I sound like someone trying to make sure you don't make a daft mistake. Someone who wants to see her boss happy. After all, you'll be less of a git to us if you get your leg over.'

Culverhouse looked at Ryan, ready to admonish her, but smiled. 'Alright. I'll message her back. But if she turns out to be a crazy cat lady with a Barry Manilow obsession I'm blaming you, alright?'

39

It was at times like this that John Lucas wished he had his mobile with him. Although he'd tried to memorise the route, Google Maps would have come in very useful.

He'd left his phone at home, knowing the police would likely be able to trace him otherwise. For all he knew, they were already tracking his movements. He knew they wouldn't have officers staking out the house, though. Not with budget cuts the way they were at the moment.

He'd picked a very specific route to Benjamin Newell's house. After he'd managed to track down his home address through an associate, he'd worked out a route using an old Ordnance Survey map – a route which would minimise his chances of being seen on the way, either by human eyes or CCTV.

When he reached the corner of Newell's road, he pulled the peak of his cap down, and pulled his hoodie tighter around his face, keeping his head low as he occasionally glanced up to check the house numbers. Once he'd got to number sixteen, he marched up the front path, took a deep breath and knocked on the door.

His head was buzzing, either from adrenaline or the half-bottle of whisky he'd drunk before coming here. He felt the muscles in his calves tensing and loosening as he bobbed on the spot, waiting for the front door of Benjamin Newell's house to open.

He waited almost a minute, watching as the hall light came on and the figure behind the door fumbled with the keys before opening the door.

As the door opened, Lucas shoulder-barged his way in, shoved Newell backwards and kicked the front door shut behind him.

Newell scrabbled backwards, trying not to lose his footing as Lucas grabbed hold of the front of his polo-shirt and pulled him back through the house, into the kitchen.

Lucas shoved him up against the kitchen worktop, Newell's head banging on the bottom of an overhead cupboard, as Lucas brought his face in close.

'Come on then. What the fuck's this all about? What the fuck are you playing at?'

'Me?' Newell replied, almost shrieking. 'You've just barged into my fucking house! What am I meant to have done?'

'You know exactly what I'm talking about,' Lucas sneered, the whisky fumes hitting Benjamin Newell square in the face. 'What is it? You still can't get over the fact you had a few months in the slammer for being thick enough to get caught? Listen. I did nearly eleven years. Eleven years.'

'You shot a fucking copper in the face!' Newell yelled.

'Yeah, and I did my time. But hey, if I hadn't done that, you wouldn't have done any time at all, would you? You would've had a fifty quid fine for driving without insurance. And that's what you couldn't let go, isn't it? You couldn't handle that you were up to your neck in it just as much as the rest of us.'

Newell tried to squirm free of Lucas's grip, but it was impossible. The man was pushing him hard against the kitchen units, the bevel of the worktop digging into the bottom of his back. He felt around behind his back with his hands, trying to do so without Lucas noticing.

'I didn't do anything,' Newell said, Lucas's grip tightening.

'Don't make me fucking laugh. Someone's tried setting me up big time here. I know it wasn't Bruno. He had no reason to. So who else is there? Oh yeah. How about the guy who blames me for him having to do bird?'

Newell's hands rested on the knife block behind him, and he felt around for the biggest carving knife he could as his eyes locked with Lucas's.

'Me, blame you? Don't flatter yourself, mate. You're the one who's spent the last eleven years whingeing about how you were going to do Footloose over the second you got out.'

'Yeah, and didn't you just know it. Perfect cover for you, eh? You knew the filth would be straight round to my gaff. Had it all worked out, didn't you?'

Lucas moved his right hand up and gripped Newell's throat, squeezing tightly.

Newell took his chance. In one smooth movement, he pulled the carving knife out of the block and brought it round, aiming to pull it straight into John Lucas's back.

Lucas spotted the movement just in time and used his arm to block Newell's movement. As the knife went clattering to the floor, Lucas grabbed hold of Newell's polo shirt again and pulled him sideways, using his right foot to swipe his legs in the opposite direction.

Within a second, Lucas was on top of him and had him pinned to the floor as Newell groped around for the knife.

'Oh, you want this, do you?' Lucas said, reaching for the knife and pinning each of Newell's arms down with his knees. 'You've realised setting me up didn't work, so now you're going to kill me. Is that it?' Lucas had the point of the knife right in Newell's face. One slight slip, and there'd be bloodshed.

'I'm telling you. I didn't set you up. I was getting married, for fuck's sake! I've had it with all that. It's in the past. I've not done nothing like that in years. I've got a wife — had a wife — and I wouldn't get involved with anything like that. I swear!'

'Yeah? And why should I believe you?'

'Because it's the truth!'

'Well you're the only person who'd want to set me up like that. I haven't spent my life trying to make enemies, you know. I've tried to get along, tried to make myself some money, tried to make a name for myself. Tried to do my old mum proud. There is no-one – no-one – who'd try to pin something like this on me. So that just leaves one possibility, doesn't it?'

Newell swallowed hard. He didn't know what Lucas was getting at. 'What?'

'You think I did it, don't you?'

Newell looked Lucas in the eyes and said nothing.

40

He didn't know whether it showed she was keen or just tragic that Christine wanted to arrange to meet up that evening. No time like the present, she'd said. That was a maxim Jack lived by, so he found it somewhat encouraging – if a little weird – that she wanted to meet up so quickly.

He'd spent the afternoon thinking about how things might pan out. It had been a long time since he'd been on a date, and he wasn't sure what to expect. Was there a different etiquette these days? He wasn't one to worry about etiquette at the best of times, but he really didn't want to mess this up. He couldn't remember the last time a woman had taken any sort of interest in him. He'd largely given up since Helen had left. Of course, for the few years preceding that he hadn't had to worry either. He'd been married – happily, he thought – so that side of his brain had been used to free up space for other stuff, much like an ageing computer hard drive.

Things would also have to be smoothed over with Emily. He'd only just got his relationship with her back on track. How would she respond to finding out her dad had moved on from her mum and got himself a new girlfriend? He didn't know, and he had no idea of the safest way to find out, either.

He'd decided to go with a casual shirt, open-necked. Wearing a suit jacket would make him feel like he was at work, and that wouldn't do him any good. He knew that if this was going to go well, he needed to completely ditch work mode and try and let his hair down for a while – what there was left of it.

That wasn't something he found easy at the best of times. Work consumed his life, and a succession of friends, colleagues and relatives had pointed out that it had a tendency to completely take over. He couldn't deny that.

He'd chosen a pub-restaurant in a village a few miles out of town. Meeting Christine in Mildenheath would be too much of a risk. For now, he wanted to keep this to himself. It wouldn't do to bump into a local criminal – or, worse, a colleague – whilst out on a first date with a woman he'd met on a mobile app. Could he even call it a date? As far as he was concerned they were just meeting up to see if they got on, but he hoped there'd be something more to it than that. Even he knew he deserved to be happy.

He'd got to the pub a good ten minutes before they'd planned to meet, and sat down at a table in the corner, absentmindedly looking through the wine list. He didn't know the first thing about wine – he used to joke that you could tell how nice it was by looking at the price column on the right hand side – but it gave him something to do while he was waiting. He didn't order her a drink as he didn't know what she wanted. She might be a wine drinker, a spirits girl or even a pint chugger. He guessed he'd find out when she turned up.

A few minutes later, he was aware of some movement in front of him, and he looked up to see a woman who looked vaguely – slightly – familiar, grinning at him and holding out a hand.

'Jack? International man of mystery?' she asked, giggling with the most annoying laugh he'd ever heard in his life.

He reached out to shake her hand. 'That's me. You must be Christine.'

'Guilty as charged!' she shrieked, holding her hands up in the air in mock surrender.

Jack forced a smile. 'Want a drink?'

'Ooh, yes please. Tomato juice for me.'

'Ah. You driving?' he said, looking back at the remaining dregs in his pint glass.

'No, no. I don't drive. I don't drink, either. No-one's going to catch me drink driving!' she said, her annoying high-pitched laugh returning.

Jack tried to look amused, and turned away towards the bar to order a tomato juice and another beer. He glanced back over to the table, where Christine was happily playing away on her phone while she waited for him. He was tempted to sneak out the side door and disappear while he could, but he at least owed it to her — and to himself — to stick around and give it a fair crack of the whip.

Once he'd got the drinks, he returned to the table, promising himself he'd try to look for the positives and not make rash judgements. Unfortunately for him, his entire career had been based on having to make quick judgements and he was finding it difficult to change the habit of a lifetime now.

'So, what do you do for a living?' he asked.

'I work in a charity shop,' she replied, not taking her eyes off her phone.

'Oh right. I didn't think they paid their staff. I thought it was voluntary.'

'It is.'

Not really what you do 'for a living', then, is it? Jack wanted to ask. 'That sounds like fun.'

'Yeah, it's alright,' Christine replied, locking her phone and placing it in between her breasts, as if they formed a makeshift pocket. 'So, what about you? Apart from being an international man of mystery, I mean.'

'I'm afraid I might have over-egged the pudding a little bit on that one.'

'You don't say.'

'If you must know, I'm a police officer. CID.'

Christine's eyebrows rose a good couple of centimetres. 'Ooh, nice,' she said, before leaning forward. 'Here, do you get to see a lot of dead bodies?'

'Erm, a few. It's all part of the job, I guess.'

'Lots of gruesome murders? Rapes?'

'Yes. Yes, a few.'

'That sort of stuff always fascinates me. I read a lot about true crime and all that. It's amazing, really, innit? I remember reading about this one bloke who used to pick up hitchhikers and kill them. Then he'd chop off their heads and boil them right down, to make stock or soup.'

I won't be going for the gazpacho, then, Culverhouse thought. 'Yeah, well thankfully those sorts of things are a rarity. Mildenheath's much more boring.' Deciding to change the subject quickly, he added: 'So, what's it like working in a charity shop?'

'It's alright,' Christine replied, taking her phone back out of her breast-pocket and replying to a text. 'You get first dibs on stuff that comes in, so that's good. Got to pay for it, mind. 'Ere, what does plaggyrism mean?'

Culverhouse looked at her, confused.

Christine showed him the phone, which he was careful not to handle. 'There, look.'

'Plagiarism,' Culverhouse replied, trying not to look or sound exasperated. 'It means stealing or copying someone else's work.'

'Fucker! Sorry, not you. My tutor texted me. Said he wants to speak to me next week about accusations of... What was it?'

'Plagiarism.'

'Yeah that.'

'What does he tutor?' Culverhouse asked.

'Oh, I'm doing a beauty course down at the college.

Couple of days a week, but it's alright. I wanna become a beauty therapist.'

Culverhouse raised his eyebrows and tried to look enthusiastic. To say her dating app profile picture had been, perhaps, a few years out of date would be accurate. He presumed she'd be no more credible a beauty therapist than would a twenty-five-stone personal trainer or a blind archery coach.

'Sounds good,' he said. 'Sorry, don't mind me. Back in two ticks.' He stood up and headed in the direction of the toilets. Once he reached the gents, he pulled his phone out of his pocket and fired off a quick text to Wendy.

Call me in five minutes. Make it sound like an emergency.

Noticing how close the toilets were to where he and Christine were sitting, he made a point of drying his already dry-hands in the noisy hand dryer before heading back out to try and put on a brave face for a little while longer.

The next few minutes were spent watching Christine type out a response to her tutor, as well as helping her to spell a number of words. He wasn't exactly a master speller himself, but this woman was missing some vital brain cells. Fortunately for him, his phone finally rang.

'Culverhouse,' he said, as he answered the call.

'Come on, then,' Wendy said on the other end of the line. 'What's this all about? I want the juicy gossip.'

'A body, you say? Where?'

'Is this the secret date that Ryan told us about but we're not meant to know about?'

Culverhouse gritted his teeth. 'Right, I think I know where that is. Do you need me there right away?'

'Let me guess. She's sixty-five, wears knitted jumpers and lives with her mum.'

'Okay, I'll head down now,' he said, standing up and fumbling to put his jacket on with his one free hand, as he mumbled 'Bitch' into the phone before hanging up. 'Sorry, I feel really bad cutting things short but I'm the on-call DCI and there's been an incident.'

'No no, no problem at all,' Christine said, grinning and doing a mock salute with her hand. 'You'd better get to the rescue.' She stood up and moved towards him. 'Let me know if it's a juicy one, though, eh?'

Before Culverhouse could realise what was happening, she was leaning in for a kiss. He managed to dodge just in time and turn it into a very brief hug.

'Right. I'll catch up with you later,' he said, as he jogged out of the pub and back towards his car. He started the engine and went to put the car into gear, but realised there was something he needed to do first. He took his phone out of his pocket, brought the screen to life and deleted the dating app.

41

John Lucas's head was starting to feel groggy after the half-bottle of whisky he'd consumed earlier. It was that horrible late-in-the-day fug you got from lunchtime drinking. There was only one way round that: carry on.

He poured himself another glass and thought about what had happened at Benjamin Newell's house. He'd not seen the man for years, but he'd barely changed. He was still the same weaselly, pathetic human being he remembered. He was the sort of person who'd mastermind stealing the Crown Jewels then get nicked for pinching a tin of Brasso to clean them.

What really irked him, though, is that Newell wouldn't deny thinking Lucas had murdered Freddie Galloway. There's no honour amongst thieves, as they say, and there was certainly none where Benjamin Newell was involved.

His head was buzzing with a thousand and one thoughts. He'd had years to get his mind straight and concentrate on the future, and all of a sudden that prospect had disappeared, replaced with having to look back into the past, back at a time he'd rather forget. It was clouded with double-crossing, lies, betrayals and he-said-she-saids. In that sort of world, the truth didn't exist. What was true to one person was completely false to another.

That was the world he'd wanted to escape from, the world he had now been thrust back into. He guessed you could never really, truly escape. Once you were marked, that was it. That history would follow you around like a bad smell, creeping back up on you when you least expected it and least wanted it to.

He knew he'd never get his chance to start again. Not properly. Just a few days ago his prospects had looked remarkably good, considering. He was able to walk out of prison and straight into a job with the shoe repairs company and he had been planning to sell the house, enabling him to set himself up somewhere on his own. Somewhere without the hassle. Somewhere without the baggage.

The job would've even allowed him to transfer to another one of their branches elsewhere in the country. Despite having thrown it all away eleven years ago, there were still people willing to give him a chance. But while the baggage of the past kept coming back to haunt him, he was in no position to take them up on those offers. He risked losing too much. He couldn't have those worlds colliding.

If truth be told, he'd love to just up sticks and go. He could do so legitimately, but that'd involve leaving a trace. If people wanted to find him, they'd find him. He'd need permission from the probation officer and he'd have to apply for that transfer at work. If he still had work to go back to, of course. Even that was a known unknown at the moment. He'd need to do it all through the official channels or he'd risk being categorised as an absconder and would be straight back in prison before he knew it.

But that wouldn't help. That wouldn't be the fresh start he needed. He'd still be looking over his shoulder everywhere he went, worrying about being betrayed, found out.

He was stuck between a rock and a hard place. He was damned if he did and damned if he didn't. As far as he saw it, there was only one way out. It wouldn't have been his favoured option, but right now it was his only one. To lose all hope and have an olive branch handed out to you – a final chance at redemption – only to have it taken away and snapped in half by the people who got you there in the first place... That hurt. That hurt a lot.

Yes, there was only one option. He had no choice. He'd made his mind up.

This was it.

42

The mood in the incident room the next morning was one of frustration. They were used to their suspects giving them seemingly credible alibis, but these ones were watertight. The problem with that was they knew the criminal code of honour meant that they tended to protect each other. A good alibi could often be too good. Suspiciously good.

The difference here was that all the main suspects weren't exactly the best of friends. They all suspected each other and didn't seem to trust anyone. But was that all an act to throw the police off the scent?

There were far too many nuances and possible double- and triple-bluffs to even begin to make sense of the situation. All they could do was strip it back down to basics and look at the facts.

'Right,' Culverhouse said, addressing the team. 'I think we might need to start looking outside the box. Let's presume our suspects' alibis are true and correct. All that means is they didn't go up to Freddie Galloway's house that night and shove half a gallon of petrol through his letterbox. It doesn't mean they weren't involved, though.'

'You mean they could've paid someone else to do it?' Steve Wing asked.

'That's exactly what I mean, yes. I think we need to look at the possibility that more people are involved somehow. Say, for instance, John Lucas is in prison and he gets talking to a fellow inmate about Galloway. He finds out they've got a mutual hatred for the man. His friend's been done over by him in the past too. Or maybe he hasn't, but he agrees to do him over in return for a bundle of cash.'

'What bundle of cash, though?' Ryan said. 'John Lucas doesn't have a pot to piss in. He was done out of the Trenton-Lowe money by Galloway too. And why would his hitman do it hours after Lucas is released from prison? Surely it'd make far more sense to do it while Lucas was still inside, so the suspicion was never going to be on him.'

'Maybe it wasn't Lucas who was involved, then,' Wendy said. 'Maybe it was Newell or Golds.'

'Not Golds,' Culverhouse said. 'He had no reason to want Galloway dead, and in any case I met the guy. He sought me out. He was absolutely cacking his pants about what had gone on, so I don't think he's involved in a million years.'

'Newell then. The timing makes sense too. Not only does Galloway end up dead, but Newell's got the perfect alibi by having his pre-wedding drinks and he gets the double-whammy of the finger of suspicion being pointed straight at John Lucas, the man whose actions got him jailed in the first place.'

Culverhouse nodded slowly. 'I've got to admit, that's probably my favourite theory at the moment. Especially with the evidence pointing to Lucas. I said from the start it looked as if it'd been set up. It was too good to be true finding all that stuff in Lucas's garage. It was almost comical.'

Ryan Mackenzie shuffled in her seat and shook her head. 'Only problem with that is there's literally no evidence pointing to Newell. It's all completely circumstantial at best. The best we've got is that he punched a bloke at his wedding.'

'He had motive,' Culverhouse replied. 'As for means and opportunity, paying someone to do it sorts both of those out.'

'Yeah, but that could be said of anyone. If that's enough to arrest and charge someone, where do you start? You'd be looking at anyone who's ever fallen out with the victim.'

'Look into his financial records, then. Work out his links and associates. There's got to be a trail somewhere.'

'More than happy to, sir, but it'll be difficult. What's the going rate for a hit? Low five figures? Maybe fifteen grand?' Ryan pulled a calculator out of her desk drawer and tapped a few buttons. 'He's been out and working for eight years or so, so that's less than two grand a year he'd need to have put aside. Eighteen-hundred and seventy-five pounds, to be precise. Or a hundred and fifty-six quid and twenty-five pence a month. I imagine most people probably draw at least that out of a cashpoint each month. It wouldn't be a difficult amount of money to hide over that period of time.'

'No, but it doesn't mean we shouldn't try looking for it,' Culverhouse replied, looking somewhat chastened. 'Besides, that hundred and fifty quid a month would be extra on top of whatever he was drawing out to buy his weekly shop and his trips to the pub or whatever.'

'I see what you're saying, sir, and we'll definitely look into it, but it'll take a lot of time and I wouldn't expect to find much. He could easily hide a grand a year through stashed cash withdrawals, plus there's the usual methods like converting it to Euros for holiday spending money, but not spending it. Keeps it under the radar. I don't imagine for one second we'll get his bank statements and see a withdrawal of fifteen grand showing up last week.'

'Let's just get the financial information and see what we can find, shall we?' Culverhouse replied through gritted teeth. That was the problem with new young officers, he thought. Always reckon they know more than the seasoned detectives who've been there and done it a thousand times before the newbies were even born. And too afraid of hard work, most of them.

He'd seen plenty drop off and opt for a change of career as soon as they realised policing was more to do with going through bank statements than running around the streets catching criminals. But the reality of it was — as much as he hated to admit it — that this was how criminals were caught. Having an arrest was one thing, but having incontrovertible evidence in black and white was something else altogether.

And it was that evidence they were sorely lacking.

Culverhouse's frustrations didn't last long, though, as there was a knock at the door, followed by a young uniformed officer, PC Karim Rashid, entering the incident room.

'Sir, sorry for interrupting your meeting. But we've just been to John Lucas's house to return some items to him after their forensic examination. We found something you might be interested in.'

43

'How the fuck did that not come up at the start?' Culverhouse yelled, as he slammed the car door behind him and started up the engine.

'I really don't know,' Wendy replied, fastening the passenger seatbelt. 'It clearly slipped through the net somewhere. We'll sort out the details later. The most important thing is that we get on it now.'

The news that PC Rashid had imparted was that when they'd gone to John Lucas's house to return his belongings, a woman had answered the door. It transpired that the woman was called Valentina Kuznetsova, and had been John Lucas's mother's cleaner for a number of years. She'd been kept on for a few hours a week after his mother had died, to keep the house clean.

'He never mentioned anything about anyone else having access to the house. He lied to us, Knight.'

'Can you be sure we even asked him? I'd have to go

back and look through the notes. It might have been overlooked.'

'Overlooked my arse. If the police find a pile of evidence from a murder in your garage and you know damn well someone else has had full access to the house for the past however many years, would you not say something? Why would he keep that from us?'

'He might not have thought of it.'

'That's bollocks and you know it. If he knows he didn't kill Freddie Galloway, and he knows the evidence from the murder scene is in his garage, he's going to bloody well think of who else might have had access to that garage. Cut and dried. If anything, that has just convinced me that John Lucas was the killer after all.'

Wendy was still less than sure. 'Let's wait and see, shall we?'

Culverhouse rang the doorbell and waited for Valentina to answer the door. When she did so, she looked to him to be the stereotypical Russian babushka – a headscarf tied around her chin and a pink apron covering the front of her dress.

She welcomed them into the house and stood in the living room as she watched the two detectives sit down.

'Please, take a seat,' Culverhouse said, feeling a little strange that he was the one trying to make her feel at home, despite the fact she'd been spending a few hours a week here for many years.

'I am afraid Mr Lucas is not here right now,' she said,

her accent still very evident, but having softened over her years in England.

'That's fine. It's you we'd like to speak to, actually,' Wendy said. 'You've been working here for a while, is that right?'

'Yes, I have many clients but John's mother, Mrs Lucas, she hired me many years ago, just before her husband died.' As she mentioned Mrs Lucas and her husband, Valentina made the sign of the cross over her chest.

'And there was provision in Mrs Lucas's will for you to keep the house clean while her son was in prison, is that right?'

'That is right, yes. Although now when John is back here, I wonder if maybe I will not work here much longer.'

'Why's that?'

'Well, I get the impression that he does not want me here. I think it is a reminder of how things used to be. I think soon he will want to sell the house.'

'He said that to you?'

'Not in so many words, no. But I have a feeling.'

The two detectives shared a glance. They both knew that 'having a feeling' didn't butter any parsnips in policing any more, despite how often that feeling tended to be right.

'And did anyone else have access to the house at all?' Culverhouse asked.

Valentina seemed to consider this for a moment, then shook her head. 'No, only John had a key, but he was in prison, and his mother before she died.'

'What about people coming into the house, though?

Not just people with keys, but anyone who might have been let in, even if only for a minute or two.'

She started to shake her head again, then stopped. 'Well yes, there was one quite recently. Maybe two weeks ago, I think. No, less. One week ago. A man came round to look at the meters for the gas and electricity. I thought it was a little bit strange because the company only came round about one month before. It is usually twice a year. When I asked him, he said there was a problem with the reading they look last time and he had to do it again.'

'And where are the meters?' Culverhouse asked.

'The gas meter is on the front wall of the house, by the holly bush. The electricity meter is in the garage.'

Both detectives tried to hide their visible shock and excitement, and briefly exchanged glances.

'Did he have anything with him?' Wendy asked her.

'Yes, a large bag. I presumed maybe this was things to fix it if he found a problem.'

The two detectives shared another glance. Both knew that meter readers weren't there to look for problems, much less to carry out repairs.

'Do you remember what he looked like?'

'Yes, a little. He was well built, maybe a little fat. I remember he was a little old for working still. Maybe he was around retirement age or he chose to work longer.'

'Hair colour?'

'Quite light, I think. Maybe going grey, but it was difficult to tell because it was a light colour anyway.'

Wendy typed a couple of words into her police-issue

tablet computer, waited for the screen to load, and showed Valentina the photograph on the screen.

'Do you recognise this man at all?'

'Yes,' Valentina said, nodding. 'Yes, that is him. That is the man who came here.'

44

'I still don't get it,' Culverhouse said, as the pair sat silently in the car outside John Lucas's house. 'Why the hell would Freddie Galloway come over to John Lucas's house, pretending to be from the gas board?'

'Well, I think we have to stick with our original theory: that our man came to the house on the pretence of reading the meters, but was actually there to plant the evidence we found when we came to speak to Lucas. Just because we now know that man was Freddie Galloway himself, that doesn't change anything.'

'But that makes no sense. You can't frame someone else for your own murder.'

'You can if it's not murder,' Wendy mumbled. She unlocked her mobile phone and called the incident room. After a few rings, DC Ryan Mackenzie answered the phone.

'Ryan, it's Wendy. Listen, can you do me a favour? We

need immediate access to Freddie Galloway's medical records. Not just the NHS ones, either. I imagine he'll have had private healthcare. You'll probably need to speak to the Patients' Association and the British Medical Association. Get onto the major private healthcare providers, too. BUPA, Spire, the lot. Get everyone on the case. We need to fast-track them urgently. Alright?'

'Sure, whatever you say.'

Wendy hung up the phone and looked at Culverhouse. They shared a look that said they both knew what the new theory was, and that the result of Ryan and the rest of the team's calls would confirm it. In exceptional circumstances, healthcare providers could provide almost instantaneous access to reports if demanded by the police. Some were better than others, though, and Wendy hoped Freddie Galloway used one of the quicker ones.

It was just under an hour before Wendy's phone rang, the familiar number on the screen letting her know it was Ryan Mackenzie calling.

'Ryan. What have you got?'

'Well, I don't know how interesting or useful it'll be to you, but it seems Freddie Galloway was seeing a private doctor. His latest records show he'd been living with liver cancer. The prognosis was that it was terminal. Looks like the poor bloke was going to be dead before long anyway. Does that help at all?'

For the first time in a few days, Wendy smiled. 'Oh yes. More than you know.'

45

Heather Bateman looked up from her mobile phone at the electronic noticeboard. Platform one at Middlebrook station was a boring place at the best of times, but there was another eighteen minutes until her train was due to arrive. She was glad it wasn't raining.

She tried to calculate how many hours she'd spent waiting on this platform. Her job meant she had to commute into London at all sorts of hours of the day. The morning rush hours weren't so bad, as the trains came through every few minutes. At other times of the day, though, you could be in for a long wait – especially if there were delays or station closures.

Heather had the unfortunate situation of living near the worst-performing train line in the country, according to official figures. Well, at least the area was finally famous for something.

She'd been a shift manager on the London Underground for almost twelve years now. It was true that the network was staffed by only two types of people: those who worked for London Underground for a very short period of time, and lifers. They said if you got past your first six months, you'd be there until the day you retired. Retirement seemed a long way off for Heather, but she could see the truth in it. It was a job you either loved or hated, and although Heather wouldn't admit it out loud, she actually quite enjoyed her job.

It was something that gave her a huge amount of variety in her days. The job was always the same, but what it threw at you changed every single day. In the past couple of days alone she'd had to help coordinate the response to a woman having a heart attack at Canning Town station, an infestation of rats at Green Park and a child whose Batman outfit had got caught in the escalator at Baker Street. It certainly wasn't a job where any two days were the same.

She looked up at the electronic noticeboard again. Sixteen minutes. She leaned back against the cold metal seat, hanging her head back over the edge as she felt the sun on her face and the top of the seat digging into the back of her neck. Only for a minute, though. She'd fallen asleep in this position on one of these seats once before after a stretch of long shifts, and couldn't get back up again. Her neck had locked into place.

Remembering this, she brought her head forward again a little sooner than planned, and looked around her for something of interest. There was never anything of interest at Middlebrook station. Situated in a village of two thousand people — most of whom lived on the far side of the village and were already at work in London by now — it was a quiet station at the best of times. Unless she was here at rush hour, she rarely saw another person on the platforms, even less often a member of staff milling about. The station was completely out in the open, and you could see for miles in either direction up and down the tracks.

It was then that the figure caught her eye, on the bridge that connected the four platforms.

She put her glasses on to get a better look, and could see that it was a man. He was standing in the middle of the bridge, looking over the edge, up the tracks. It was an odd thing to be doing, she thought. There were occasionally trainspotters at the station, but they usually worked in pairs and stood on the platforms with cameras. This man just appeared to be peering over the edge, motionless.

She noticed movement further up the tracks, on one of the fast tracks. On this line, platforms one and three were southbound; two and four northbound. Two and three, the middle lines, were for fast, overtaking trains which only stopped at a handful of stations along the line — usually in the cities and major towns.

The train barely seemed to be moving at all — an optical illusion, she knew, as she was watching it from an almost head-on position. She knew the train would actually be doing well in excess of eighty miles an hour.

Just as she noticed the train, she heard the automated station announcement over the tannoy.

The train now approaching platform three does not stop here. Please stand well clear from the edge of platform three.

Heather watched as, far from keeping clear of the edge of anything, the man hung his arms over the top of the bridge and hoisted himself up, swinging a leg up onto the top of the wall before clambering onto his knees. She looked on in horror, frozen to the spot, knowing exactly what was going on, as the man slowly and carefully got to his feet.

She knew the breeze would be strong up there, even though the air was still at platform level. She watched as the man put his arms out to the side to steady himself, waiting for the perfect moment.

She broke free from her terror and shouted out. 'No! Stop!'

The man turned his head in the direction of the noise, saw Heather, and turned his head back to look up the train line as Heather watched the train hurtle down the track towards him.

46

John Lucas swallowed hard as he felt his legs wobble beneath him. He looked down at the steel rails, wooden sleepers and chipped stone beneath him.

So this was it. This was where it all ended. This was to be his final resting place. Or, more accurately, some of him would rest more or less below where he now stood and other parts of him would be spread along the track and the front of the train – if he timed the jump right.

He knew what was going to happen and he knew it wouldn't be pretty. But right now he didn't care. Yeah, the train driver would need counselling and might never work again, but as far as John was concerned he could go fuck himself. He didn't care about anything any more. He didn't even care about his own life, never mind that of some bloke driving a train.

It would hurt. He knew that. But it would only be for a split second, if that. His skull would almost instantly crack or blow open, leaving him completely braindead within a second at the very most. It would be instantaneous relief from this life.

That word made him laugh. Life. It hadn't been a life. He'd been dragged up on a shitty estate and had fallen into a world of crime – something he'd later found out he wasn't particularly good at. He'd spent his time inside looking back rather than forwards, always thinking about the stupid mistakes he'd made, the things he'd done and wished he hadn't. He could've started writing a list on the day he was banged up and still be writing it now.

He was a man who always seemed to make the wrong decision. He didn't know why; it was just something that happened. And each of those decisions had, in turn, led to him standing on the edge of the bridge at Middlebrook station, staring at a train he'd never seen before, but which he knew was about to end his life.

There was no point in trying any other way. All he'd ever had in life was his mum – the one person who'd really cared for him.

He'd never known close family, other than her. When his mum had become pregnant not long after leaving school, her family had disowned her. His father was a married man, a friend of the family. He never knew his name. He didn't want to. John had assumed for many years that he'd grown up on a council estate because that was his place in life.

He thought, like so many of his friends' families, that this was his background. It was only years later that his mum had told him she'd actually been from quite a well-off family, but on being disowned when falling pregnant she'd been forced into council housing just to put a roof over her and her son's heads.

She was as astonished as anyone to find out that her Aunt Iris had left her a decent inheritance. Not a fortune, but enough to enable her to buy her own house and set her and John up with the life she'd wanted him to have. John had his own theories on that one. In his mind, his father had been Iris's husband, his great-uncle Frank.

His mum had mentioned something in passing about Frank being a not particularly pleasant man. The inference was that he was physically abusive towards Iris. John wondered whether Frank had raped his mother — Frank's niece — and that John himself had been the product of that crime. That would, in his mind, explain why Iris had left her estate to his mum. Perhaps it was her way of apologising, of ensuring that John — her step-son, to all intents and purposes — had a half-decent upbringing.

They'd moved out of the council estate and into their own house when John was thirteen. By then, the damage had already been done.

He wondered how much of it was down to that upbringing and what was in the genes. To exist purely because one of the vilest of crimes had occurred had to affect you in some way.

In any case, it was all irrelevant. That sad, shitty little life would all be over in a few seconds. He'd be able to join his mum, wherever she was, and ask her to tell him everything. He wondered if at the moment of his death he'd suddenly know it all anyway, ascend to some all-knowing plane where everything becomes clear. That was the thing about death – no-one really knew what happened. There was no way of coming back and telling everyone what it was like. No-one would ever know until it happened to them.

Whatever it was like, it would be infinitely preferable to living this shitty life.

He looked down over the edge again, the tips of his toes protruding over the precipice as he started to hear the train rushing down the tracks.

He swallowed again, then heard a voice behind and below him. He turned round to look and saw a woman on the far platform, looking shocked and panicked.

He turned his head back towards the train and scrunched his eyes shut tight.

47

The major incident room at Mildenheath CID was buzzing as Jack Culverhouse updated the team on what they'd discovered. Steve Wing was the first to ask questions.

'What, so he decided that rather than let the cancer get him, he'd rather die in a house fire and frame someone else for it? That don't make sense to me, guv.'

'He didn't die in a house fire, though, did he? He died from jumping off the balcony and hitting the slabs.'

Culverhouse watched as the cogs whirred in Steve's brain, a gradual look of realisation creeping across his face.

'So you're saying that Galloway was never trying to escape the fire? Jesus. He was never aiming for the pool, was he? He always intended to hit the deck and die quickly and painlessly.'

'Exactly. Think about it. This is the kind of guy whose whole life has been built on pride. That's what everything is about as far as he's concerned. He's proud he's still doing well, proud of his beautiful house. Then a doctor tells him he's dying and he can't do a thing about it. That's not how blokes like Freddie Galloway bow out. They do things their own way. Always in control, right to the last. He worked hard for that house as far as he was concerned, and he was going to take it with him. If he was going to die, he was going to do it his way and take the lot with him.'

'The problem we've got,' Wendy said, 'is proving it. I don't imagine any of the items in John Lucas's garage will have Galloway's DNA on them, but we'll check against all known samples. We might be able to track down the purchase of the jerry can and trainers, but even if we do I very much doubt if Freddie Galloway himself nipped out to the shops to buy them. He'd have one of his men do it for him.'

'If they were bought by someone we can link to Galloway, that could do it,' Ryan said.

'True, but it's all circumstantial again. The way I see it, the situation is this. All signs point to John Lucas. But we can't prove for definite Lucas was at the scene. It seems extraordinarily unlikely he would've been stupid enough to do something like that, and I for one believe him. I've sat opposite enough people in interview rooms to have a fairly decent idea over whether someone's guilty or not. As we all know only too well, it's not about working out whether someone's guilty. That's the easy bit. It's about proving it. Now, we can't prove something *didn't* happen, so we'd have to prove that something else *did*. For that we'll need to hammer the forensics. I've got a few ideas on that front.'

'Nice one, Knight,' Culverhouse said. 'We'll have a chat about that. Ryan, did you get anything on Newell's financials?'

'Yes and no,' Ryan replied. 'The guy barely uses cash at all, it seems. Everything is paid for on his debit card. He does take cash out occasionally, but rarely any more than thirty quid a month. Even at that, you're talking less than four grand over eleven years – and that's assuming every penny he withdrew was for the hitman. I don't think you'd find many people who'd do a hit for that.'

'Romanians might,' Steve said.

'Trust me, Steve. If we were looking at a four-grand hitman's work, we'd know about it by now,' Culverhouse replied.

He was interrupted by the sound of his work mobile phone ringing. The number on the screen told him it was the operational command centre.

'Culverhouse,' he said, answering the phone.

'Sir, we've just had a call from a commuter at Middlebrook station who reported a man threatening to throw himself off the bridge.'

'Right, well you'll have to send uniform in. There are negotiators they can call in who—'

'No, sir. Sorry. He's not there any more. He climbed down from the bridge after she called out to him, then legged it. But she saw him take his mobile out of his pocket and throw it down onto the tracks. There was a train coming in, but the phone fell between the lines and didn't get damaged. They managed to get the lines deactivated while they retrieved it. The phone had a passcode lock, but they could see from the signal indicator that the phone was on the Tesco Mobile network. Because they were worried for the man's safety and didn't have an ID on him, they got the network to identify the owner of the mobile. It was the only phone on Tesco Mobile within the vicinity of the station, and they matched it to Mr John Lucas.'

'Christ,' Culverhouse said, glad he'd held on and not just hung up the phone when the rambling explanation started. 'And where is he now?'

'No idea, sir. Units are out looking for him as there are safety concerns about him, but according to the eyewitness he ran towards the station building. By the time units arrived at the scene, he was nowhere to be found.'

Culverhouse tried to form a picture of Middlebrook station in his mind's eye. 'There's a cab office there, isn't there? In the station building. Get onto them and find out if they took a fare from a man matching John Lucas's description. In the meantime, keep scouring the area. I'll see if we can get Hotel Oscar Nine Nine up with thermal imaging. There's a lot of woodland and scrubland around there. Oh fuck,' he said, bringing his palm to his forehead.

'What is it, sir?'

'He's only a mile or two away from the motorway junction, there. If he didn't get any luck with the railway bridge, there's a decent chance he might be heading for the road bridge over the motorway.'

48

John Lucas handed a twenty-pound note over to the cab driver and climbed out onto the pavement.

He didn't know why, but he'd had the good sense to bring his wallet out with him earlier. Maybe it was a subconscious bit of assistance for whoever would have had the grisly job of identifying his body. A little helping hand for the police. Well, that was totally out of the question now.

The police were getting no favours from him. He'd spent his whole life being fucked over by the police. If that stupid officer hadn't turned up while he was leaving Trenton-Lowe, if that idiot hadn't pulled Peter over, if the twats in CID had worked out that he was obviously being fitted up...

Life was all ifs and buts. And now he couldn't even end it all himself. He was doomed, destined to stay on this bloody planet, in this pitiful existence. And there was nothing he could do about it.

Except he knew exactly what he was going to do.

He was going to show them what was what. He was going to let them know exactly what they'd done to him.

He knew he wouldn't have long before they'd start crawling round here. He'd chucked his phone onto the tracks so they wouldn't be able to trace his movements, but he knew they would have identified it as his phone before too long. Then they'd be swarming round here like mosquitoes, baying for blood, ready to suck out even more of his soul.

He opened the front door, marched through to the kitchen and twisted open the cap on the bottle of whisky. He threw his head back and took five or six big glugs. It was enough to make him feel instantly sick, but he swallowed that feeling back down with the realisation of what was to come.

He walked over to the other side of the room, picked the carving knife out of the knife block and ran his finger over the blade.

Good. It was sharp.

49

Back in the major incident room, the team were eagerly awaiting more news. There wasn't much they could do – dog units were out on the ground and Hotel Oscar Nine Nine, the regional police helicopter, could be in the air within minutes. But first they needed to know whether Lucas was on foot or not.

Culverhouse had held out on requesting the chopper, knowing there was a chance Lucas would have used the taxi firm at the station. He didn't have a car of his own, and he would have had to rely on another form of transportation to reach Middlebrook in the first place. It wasn't on the major bus routes, so that only left taxis or favours from friends. And it wasn't often people called a friend for a lift to go and kill themselves.

Once he heard back that Lucas hadn't taken a taxi, he'd have the chopper in the air. Until then he'd have to hang fire, knowing it would cost the force a lot of money to engage Hotel Oscar Nine Nine and that the Police and Crime Commissioner would have his guts for garters if it was sent up unnecessarily.

The phone on the desk in the middle of the incident room rang, and Culverhouse immediately jabbed the speakerphone button so the rest of the team could hear.

'Culverhouse.'

'Sir, we've got Mrs Wilson in reception. She wants to see a detective, she says. She thinks her next-door neighbour is breeding spy dogs for the Russians.'

'Jesus Christ. Steve, get down there and do the dance, will you?' Culverhouse barked.

'Not me, guv. I went last time. I think it's your turn, actually.'

Culverhouse's face told Steve everything he needed to know about his reaction to that.

'Do you not think I'm a bit fucking busy here?'

'I'll go,' Wendy said, standing up. 'I need the loo anyway.'

A few seconds after Wendy had left the room, the phone rang again. Again, Culverhouse jabbed the speakerphone button and stated his name.

'Sir, we've had an update from officers at the scene. The taxi company confirmed that a driver left about twenty minutes ago with a man who matches Lucas's description. Said he wanted to be dropped off in Mildenheath, but gave no specific address.'

Culverhouse let out a huge sigh.

'Right. Get onto the driver and find out where he's

dropping him off. In the meantime, get units round to Lucas's home address. That's where he's likely to be going. In fact, I'll go too. I'll take DS Wing and DC Mackenzie with me. Twenty minutes, did you say? That might even give us time to cut him off if the traffic was bad. There's a decent chance he might not have got back yet. We can be there in three or four minutes.' Culverhouse ended the call and turned to Steve Wing and Ryan Mackenzie, who'd already heard what he'd said and were putting on their jackets. 'Right, you two. Let's get moving.'

50

Alfie Little sat on the cold metal bench and sipped at a cup of sweet tea. He'd never had a jumper before. He was the only one on his shift who hadn't, in fact.

One of the things that was drilled into him while he was training was that he'd almost certainly come across a situation like this, but no number of fair warnings could ever prepare you for it. He was shaking as he recounted what he saw to the police constable, who was jotting it all down in his notepad.

He was just glad the guy hadn't actually jumped. If Alfie had reacted so badly to that close call, what would have happened if the guy had gone through with it, fallen through the air and smashed into the front of the speeding train, exploding in a bloody mess?

Fortunately, he'd seen the man on the bridge as he approached the station and had immediately begun to slow the train down. It had eventually stopped almost a hundred yards past the station. He'd seen the man throw something onto the tracks, and had a duty to stop the train and report the incident immediately. That would ensure that no other trains would pass through the station, and would instead be halted a few hundred yards shy of it.

Another police constable, a woman, came over to speak to the man who was taking his statement.

'Karim, we've just had an update. He took a cab from here into Mildenheath. Driver dropped him off round the corner from where he lives. They're en route to his home address as we speak. They're pulling back the search units.'

'Sounds like he's gone home,' PC Rashid said to Alfie Little. 'Looks like it might be his and your lucky day.'

Alfie raised his eyebrows and blinked a few times. It certainly didn't feel very lucky to him.

51

John Lucas ran his finger along the blade of the carving knife inside his jacket pocket, the baseball cap pulled down low over his face, as he stood outside the Prince Albert pub, the building next door to Mildenheath Police station.

He could feel the whisky running through him, making him breathe heavily. It hadn't dulled the anger at all. Nothing ever would now. He'd been wronged too many times, and this time it was his turn to try and make things right. Because no-one else was going to bother.

He didn't care what happened afterwards. They could bang him up for the rest of his life for all he cared. What use was it being out here, anyway? He'd been safer on the inside. He'd known who to trust and who not to trust, known there were people there employed to watch out for his safety. Out here there was nothing.

He knew the police just wanted to see him go down again. They were pissed off that one of their own had been shot all those years ago. They were like that, the police. Tribal. If you so much as looked the wrong way at one, the others would be on you like a ton of bricks. They didn't do forgiving and forgetting. They did constant revenge, persistant reminders. And he was never going to be allowed to move on from what had happened eleven years ago, what had happened since.

So what was the point? If you were never allowed to move on from injuring one officer — despite showing plenty of remorse when required — why not take out more of the pigs? He had nothing to lose. And it was their own stupid fault that they'd put him in this position. They'd given him no option. And they were about to realise that was very stupid indeed.

He took a deep breath, adjusted the peak on his cap, took a firm grip of the knife inside his jacket pocket and walked towards the front doors of the police station.

'Mrs Wilson, I promise you absolutely we'll look into it for you. I've got it all here: Russian spy dogs, radio signal interference, switching your TV on to find it tuned to Russia Today. I must admit it sounds very compelling. We'll get straight onto it.'

Wendy looked over Mrs Wilson's shoulder as she spoke, meeting the eye of the civilian officer on the front desk, who was trying her best not to laugh out loud.

Mrs Wilson signalled that she was happy with that response and remarked that she expected to see a dawn raid on her neighbour's property. Wendy knew she would have forgotten all about having even made this report by dawn tomorrow, so she nodded and smiled, vaguely aware of the sound of the front door to the police station opening behind her.

He looked down at the ground as he walked in, but tried not to look too suspicious. Closing the door behind him, he looked up, seeing two people in front of him.

One was some doddery old bitch with a walking stick, and the other looked somewhat familiar. She was clearly a copper, so he guessed she could be any one of a... No. He knew exactly who it was now. It was that cow of a detective who'd interviewed him after he was arrested for the fire at Freddie Galloway's.

Oh yes. This was just too good to be true. This was perfect. This was the ideal way to take a stand and go down in a blaze of glory. It was beautiful.

As the old woman started to walk towards the exit, the detective woman headed towards a door that seemed to lead to the back of the station, protected by an electronic key fob and number pad.

He decided he needed to take his chance now.

He ran towards her, shoved her against the door, and brought his left arm around her throat, dragging her back into the waiting area, the blade of the knife digging into the side of her neck.

52

Culverhouse arrived at John Lucas's house as the first response officers were lifting the enforcer out of the back of the van. The enforcer, a huge metal battering ram, was used to force entry to properties by bashing the door in.

'Steve, get round the back in case he escapes that way. Ryan, follow me.' He marched up to the front of the house and showed his ID card to the officers. 'DCI Culverhouse, Mildenheath CID. This is DC Mackenzie. Any signs of life in there?'

'Not taking any chances, sir. We're happy to force entry immediately if you are.'

Culverhouse ran through the protocol in his mind. Lucas was a previous offender with a history of violence, particularly towards police officers. He'd shown signs of being psychologically unstable within the past half an hour. They didn't know for certain he was in the house, but there was a pretty decent chance — especially as he'd had the taxi drop him off just around the corner.

'I'm happy to authorise that,' he replied, agreeing with the officer that they couldn't afford to take any chances. 'Stand back,' he said to Ryan, as they gave the officer carrying the enforcer ample space to swing.

On the second strike, the wooden door flew open and banged against the wall inside. The officer carrying the enforcer stepped aside, with Culverhouse entering first, followed by Mackenzie and the other officers. This wasn't strictly according to protocol, but Culverhouse had been trained for these events many moons ago, and was determined to be the man to nab John Lucas himself.

He yelled 'Police!' at the top of his voice, as did the others. It was a surprisingly effective tactic, which tended to result in the occupants panicking and freezing on the spot. You could usually tell when there were people in a house that you'd forced entry to, and Culverhouse didn't like the feel of this one.

They pushed open the doors to each room and had a good look around, but it quickly became apparent that John Lucas was nowhere to be seen.

Culverhouse walked through to the back of the house and into the kitchen. There was a whisky bottle on the worktop, its lid sitting next to it. He looked at the bottle more closely.

'He's been here very recently,' he called out to Ryan Mackenzie, who came to join him in the kitchen. 'Look.' He pointed to the neck of the bottle, which had a small trickle of whisky running down the outside of the bottle, where it had already reached the label and soaked in. 'It's still wet. We must've just missed him.'

Ryan looked at the bottle. 'So he's come home and taken a mouthful of whisky out of the bottle. Then what? Where's he gone?'

Culverhouse looked around the kitchen for anything else that might give them a clue. His eyes locked on the knife block.

'Where's his dishwasher?' he asked.

'Don't know. Don't think he's got one,' Ryan said, looking around. 'Why's that?'

'Because there's a knife missing from this bloody big gap in the knife block. And there isn't one in the sink.'

Before they got any further, a uniformed officer came jogging into the kitchen, clutching his radio.

'Sir. We've just had a call from the station.'

53

'Put the knife down, sir. You're in a police station,' Liz Shipton called from behind the front desk. She'd been trained to know how to deal with a situation like this, but it wasn't something she'd expected to see.

In the case of someone kicking off in reception, there was a button which would alert officers around the station, summoning them for assistance. This wasn't an option Liz wanted to take in this instance. Any sign of a commotion and the man could plunge the knife into DS Knight's neck within a millisecond.

Officers were often reminded how to deal with situations such as these. The current terrorism threat level meant they were always hyper-aware of what to do should someone enter a police station or public area and take a hostage or threaten to blow themselves up. Going in all guns blazing just wouldn't do.

But if Liz pushed the panic button there would be the

best part of a dozen officers in the room within a couple of seconds, and she had no way of knowing how the man would react to that. She decided, within a fraction of a second, that gentle negotiation might be the only way to save DS Knight's life.

'I know where I am,' the man replied. 'And I know who this bitch is, too.'

'John, you don't need to do anything silly,' Wendy said, her voice sounding strained and nervous.

'Yeah? Give me one good reason why I shouldn't shove this knife right through your fucking neck,' he sneered, alcohol fumes making Wendy blink and retch.

'Because you don't need to,' she said, struggling to stay calm and not get Lucas any more agitated than he already was. 'Is this because we interviewed you over Freddie Galloway's death?'

'Don't flatter yourself,' Lucas said, unconvincingly. 'All my life I've been shat on. Everywhere I turn, every time something is going well in my life, you lot turn up and piss on my fucking bonfire. And I'm sick of it!'

Lucas's voice raised to a shout, and Wendy felt a small trickle of blood start to run down the side of her neck as the increased pressure from the blade pierced the skin.

'Do you have any idea what that's like? That fucking idiot turning up at Trenton-Lowe. You lot have never forgiven me for that. You never will. I didn't ask him to come, did I? That was his own bloody fault. Then Galloway fucked us all over and swanned off to his bloody mansion while I rotted in jail. And then what happens?

Someone does what we've all wanted to do and burns his house to the ground, on the day I get out of fucking prison! Well, what do you know? Your lot are round at my door again. I was a free man for not even twenty-four hours, and you've got me back in a cell. 'Cos you just can't get over it, can you? You can't get over the fact that your mate was stupid enough to turn up on his own that night. So at every chance you get, you're going to try to make sure I suffer.'

'That's not true, John,' Wendy said.

'How'd all that shit get in my garage, hmm? Who put it there? Was it you or the fat one?'

'John, we know you didn't kill Freddie Galloway. We know you didn't set fire to his house.'

'Oh yeah? Don't give me that bollocks. I know you've been sniffing around still. The bloody cleaner told me you'd been round again, so don't give me that.'

'It's true,' Wendy said, her voice shaking as she started to feel the pain of the blade inside her raw flesh. 'We know you've been set up, John. And we know who by.'

Lucas stayed silent for a moment, seeming to consider this. 'Go on then,' he said, eventually. 'Who?'

'Put the knife down and I'll tell you, John. It's something we need to discuss properly.'

Lucas snorted and used his left hand to yank Wendy's hair back.

'Wrong answer,' he said, as he shoved the knife into her neck.

54

Liz Shipton pushed the panic button the second she realised the situation had escalated, and within seconds the Station Duty Office was full of police officers who'd streamed out of the rooms behind at the sound of the alarm.

She watched on helplessly as 'Panic alarm SDO! Panic alarm SDO!' rang out over the tannoy system at an ear-piercing volume as half a dozen officers tackled John Lucas to the ground and disarmed him. Two officers were attending to DS Knight, one of them attempting to stem the bleeding with his hands whilst another grabbed the police-issue bandages from the pouch on his belt.

'Lima Alfa one four six. Officer with a stab wound to the neck in SDO. Ambo needed, over.'

'Get off! Get the fuck off me!'

'Nick, we'll need more bandages. It's not stopping.'

'Claire, take his legs. Get him immobilised.'

'Fucking hell, this is bad.'

'Get off me!'

The officers manhandled John Lucas out through the front entrance and round towards the custody suite, where Liz knew he'd be arrested and booked into a cell.

Control would have called an ambulance already, which'd be on its way. Judging by the amount of blood that was now on the floor of the duty office, Liz wondered whether it could get here quickly enough. There was an ambulance station less than half a mile away, but sometimes that didn't mean a thing. A neck wound could be almost instantly fatal.

She could swear she heard a faint gurgling sound coming from DS Knight, but it was difficult to hear anything over the commotion. She could only watch on in horror, stunned into motionless silence as she watched DCI Culverhouse and two other CID officers rush in through the front doors of the building.

55

'Don't move,' were the first words Wendy heard. 'It's okay. You're in safe hands.'

She blinked as the bright lights seared her eyeballs. She tried to speak, but the pain was unbearable.

'It's okay. Don't try to speak. You're in Mildenheath General Hospital, Wendy. My name's Rosie Ashton, I'm one of the nurses here. You've had a bit of a battle on your hands but you're through the worst of it.'

Wendy tried to recall what had happened. Her mind was hazy in many ways and she couldn't seem to keep hold of any thought for long. She guessed she was probably on some form of medication. She remembered the smell of alcohol, an arm around her neck, the slight trickle of blood.

She heard footsteps growing louder as someone approached the bed from the corridor outside.

'Fuck's sake. Two days I've spent sitting here watching

you lie there dribbling. I nip out for a quick piss and *now* you choose to bloody wake up.'

That voice sounded familiar, Wendy thought. It certainly wasn't a nurse.

She looked at Culverhouse and tried to express a message with her eyes, but wasn't getting anywhere.

'Get this,' the DCI said, walking over to her bed. 'I think I've got it memorised now. An incision between the posterior and middle scalene muscles with damage to the sternocleidomastoid and abrasion of the common carotid. What do you make of that, matron?'

'I'm a nurse,' Rosie said. 'And very good.'

'Basically, it'll hurt like fuck and you've lost a lot of blood but we won't need to pay for a funeral, so that's a bonus.'

Rosie smiled. 'Personally I'd word it a little differently. You've been very lucky, Wendy. You're not totally out of the woods yet, but you're a good ninety-five percent of the way there. They managed to repair the artery and stop the bleeding, which was substantial. They've had to give a partial transfusion, so you're not going to be feeling great for some time. The muscles in your neck are going to need you to rest and relax. You've got a brace on so you can't do them any major damage, but if I were you I wouldn't try.'

'Pretty drastic way of trying to get out of your inspector's exams, though.'

Wendy closed her eyes. She was still struggling to come to terms with what had happened to her, and was a long way from being able to cope with the thought that her chances of taking the exams were over for another year. There'd be time off work, a recovery period, sick leave, a return-to-work medical...

As if being stabbed in the neck wasn't enough, she'd now have to jump through any number of hoops before she was able to even sit down and do her job again.

She lifted her hand and made a writing motion.

'You want a pen and paper?' the nurse asked.

Wendy did a long blink to indicate that was exactly what she wanted.

'Okay, but you'll have to be careful. You need to keep your head and neck still. Here we go,' she said, positioning the raised, slanted surface in front of Wendy.

Wendy lifted the pen and started to write on the paper. It took far more effort than she expected.

How long will I be here?

The nurse smiled. 'Until the doctors are satisfied you're safe to go home. You've sustained quite a serious injury.'

Where's Lucas?

Rosie signalled to Culverhouse that this was one for him to answer.

'In a cell. Crown Prosecution Service have recommended a charge of attempted murder. He'll be off to a remand prison within the next day or so. I can't see him getting anything other than the maximum sentence. He's attempted to kill two police officers now. I hope the bastard rots.'

Op Mandible?

'Don't you worry about that. There've been developments and we're about ready to close the case, but there's plenty of time for you to catch up on all that. You just worry about getting better, alright?'

Wendy did another two-second blink, and forced a small, painful smile.

'Oh, and don't switch the telly on,' Culverhouse added. 'Not unless you want any more swelling around your head area. You're all over the news channels. Half of them are reporting it as a "suspected terrorist incident". Bloody idiots. Can hardly see John Lucas as an Al-Qaeda suicide bomber, can you?'

Wendy tried not to laugh, knowing it would hurt.

A thought crossed her mind. She reached for the pen and paper again.

Cookie?

'I think you need to worry about yourself more than a sodding cat, but yes, it's being taken care of. Next time you might want to leave a spare key with a friend or neighbour. You owe me eighty quid for a new lock on your front door.'

You kicked it in?

'Didn't have much choice,' Culverhouse said. 'Bloody thing needed feeding, didn't it? I got my own back, though. I fed him the fillet steak I found in your fridge.'

Again, Wendy tried not to laugh. A large part of her hoped she'd be in hospital for quite some time to come. At least it'd keep her away from the baying press pack until all the fuss had died down.

After that, a desk-bound inspector's job was starting to look quite appealing.

56

Back at the station, Culverhouse entered the custody suite and asked the custody sergeant if he could see John Lucas.

He was taken through to Lucas's cell, the officer lifting the metal privacy flap down to check inside before unlocking the door and letting Culverhouse inside.

He stepped into the cell and waited as the door was closed and locked behind him.

John Lucas was sitting on the thin blue plastic mattress he could call his bed, feet up on the bed and knees in the air as he rested his back and head against the cold brick wall.

Culverhouse stood and looked at him for almost a minute, neither of them saying a word, both of them knowing what the other was thinking. Although there was silence, a thousand words were said.

It was Culverhouse who eventually broke the deadlock.

'Forensics found traces of accelerant on Galloway's

hands. Both the police and the fire service are happy that Galloway set fire to his own house.'

Lucas looked at him for a few moments.

'Why?'

'We did some computer-modelled reconstructions on the house and pool area,' Culverhouse said, ignoring him. 'He could have easily reached the pool from that balcony. He was in decent enough health to make the jump. There were no marks on the balcony or on his legs that indicated that he'd slipped when jumping. He deliberately aimed to miss the pool and hit the patio, knowing he'd die instantly rather than burn to a slow death in the house.'

'But why?' Lucas asked again, shaking his head slowly.

'He was riddled with cancer. He wanted to be in charge of his own destiny. And he wanted to take you down at the same time.'

'Why would he do that?'

'That's for you to live with. That's a question I hope you ask yourself every day. I hope it troubles you for the rest of your life. But maybe, just maybe he couldn't quite forgive you for fucking up that night eleven years ago.'

'Me? He was the one who gave us duff information and ran off with all the money!'

Culverhouse shook his head. 'I don't think he did. We don't know where that money went, but we're pretty sure it didn't go to him. It's not easy to hide half a million quid in cash. We reckon Galloway's inside man at Trenton-Lowe was the managing director. The company had been doing alright before the gypsy camp deal. Not great, but okay. He must've been shitting himself at what might happen if he got too heavily involved with those people. He'd probably heard all the stories. I presume you didn't know he'd been living out his retirement in a lovely little villa in Portugal, did you? No, us neither. Bought for not far off half a million quid, four years after the robbery.'

Lucas swallowed. 'So they did us all over. Galloway and the Trenton-Lowe guy.'

'Galloway got away with as little from that job as the rest of you did. He can't have known the bloke had hidden the money then run off to Portugal with it. Until his dying day, he believed the failure of that job was down to you. As far as he was concerned, you cost him half a million quid.'

'But why? I've not got a pot to piss in!'

'We don't know. We never will. But there are a few things we do know. We know you drew police attention to Galloway like flies to shit when you pulled that trigger. As far as I'm concerned, you should be banged up permanently for that. We know Galloway was an old school criminal, a man who didn't touch women, children or police officers. We know you very publicly swore that you were going to get your revenge on Galloway when you got out. And it looks to me like he got there before you did. Call it a pre-emptive strike, if you will. He was dying anyway, so why not take control over when and how, and ensure you go back inside for another decade or two just to top things off? And the most beautiful part of all of it is that you could've walked free. You were an innocent man on that front, about to be vindicated. But then you went and did something *really* fucking stupid and bollocksed it all up. That's your legacy. That's the story of your life. And you know what? I feel sorry for you.'

Culverhouse turned and knocked on the door to indicate that he wanted to be let out.

'How long am I going down for?' Lucas said, his voice barely a whisper and cracking with tears.

Culverhouse spoke without turning as he waited for the officer to open the door.

'Right now, I really couldn't give a shit.'

57

Tyrone unlocked the main door to the block of flats and headed off down the road in the direction of the boxing club.

He was still nowhere near fully recovered, but he wasn't the sort of guy who could go long without getting back to action. He figured a few light rounds with a punchbag couldn't do him any harm. Anyway, he'd stop if the pain got too much.

He'd barely covered thirty yards when he remembered he'd forgotten his phone. Fishing into his pocket for his keys again, he turned and headed back, and saw Elijah – his sister's boyfriend – letting himself in through the main door.

There was nothing strange in that itself – Elijah had a key of his own – but something didn't feel right. Rather than call out, he waited for Elijah to enter the building, then jogged up the front steps, waited a few seconds and let himself in. Elijah, like Tyrone, always took the stairs, so Tyrone made sure to hang back a bit to ensure he wasn't seen on the way up.

Once Elijah was out of view on their floor, Tyrone jogged up the last few stairs and rounded the corner, giving himself a full view of the front door to their flat. He'd expected to see Elijah letting himself in with his key, but what he saw was something completely different.

Elijah was crouched down on one knee, and appeared to be pushing something under the door to the flat.

'What's going on?' Tyrone said, before immediately realising the implication.

Before he could stop himself, he'd launched himself at Elijah the moment he'd spun around and pinned him against the front door, his forearm pressed across Elijah's throat.

'It was you, wasn't it? That message through the door. The texts. It was all you.'

Elijah made a gurgling noise that told Tyrone he was pressing too hard for him to be able to speak. Tyrone loosened his grip.

'I dunno what you're talking about, man. I just came back to get some stuff.'

'Bullshit. I saw you just now, kneeling down.'

'I dropped my key.'

'What, so if I open that door right now there's not gonna be another bit of paper with a threat on it? That what you're saying? 'Cos I just left this place not two minutes ago. You know I did, 'cos you was watching me, weren't you? You waited til I went out, then snuck up here. That's how you got out so quick last time, too. You know the place as well as I do.'

Elijah said nothing in response, but Tyrone could see his suspicions were right.

'Who told you? How'd you find out?' Tyrone asked.

'People talk, bruv. You know what it's like around here.'

'What, and you've got a problem with it? Yeah, I'm gay. So what? And you know what? I don't give a shit any more. I'm not going to spend my life pretending I'm something I'm not, just because of little dicks like you. So you don't like living in the same flat as a gay guy? What, you think I'm going to just bend you over in the shower or something? Let me tell you something, bruv. You're as likely to get hit on by a gay guy as you are a straight woman. And that ain't gonna happen either, 'cos you're a wasteman. You ain't done nothing for us. This is my flat, you get me? And you go and treat me like that? You make me sick. It weren't even you who jumped me, was it?'

Elijah shook his head.

'No. But you put them up to it. Couldn't even do your own dirty work. You're pathetic.'

Tyrone gave Elijah one last shove, then stepped back and wiped the spittle from his mouth with his sleeve.

'So what now?' Elijah said, after a few seconds. 'I can try and find myself a new place. Might not take too long if the council can sort me out. I'd technically be homeless, so I should get priority.'

Tyrone let our a small laugh. 'Don't think you're getting

away that easy. There's no way in hell I'm kicking you out. I'm not taking the easy road, bruv. You're staying here. You're going to live in the same flat as a gay guy and you're going to put up with it. You're going to bring my nephew up the way he deserves, the way my sister deserves. Whether you tell her what you are and what you've done, that's up to you. That's up to your conscience. If you've got one.'

Tyrone turned around and headed for the stairs. He was just about ready for that punchbag now.

58

THREE WEEKS LATER

Wendy was jolted from her painkiller-induced light sleep by the sound of her doorbell. She barely registered the antiques auction programme on the TV before muting it, rising to her feet and heading slowly towards the front door.

She looked through the spyhole and recognised the person in front of her immediately. She opened the door.

'Xav. What are you doing here?' she said, her voice sounding strained.

'I heard what happened to you. Well, that sounds stupid. Everyone heard what happened to you. But, I mean, I wanted to give you a bit of space and time after getting home before... Well, I just wanted to say hi.'

Wendy smiled and let out a small laugh. 'Come in, Xav.'

He followed her inside, through the hallway and into the small but well-decorated living room.

'So, how are you bearing up?' he asked, sitting down in an armchair.

'I've been better.'

'You've looked better, too.'

'You know I can just kick you back out again, right? I've not lost my fighting skills.'

'Pity you didn't use them a few weeks back. Then you wouldn't need that daft thing round your neck.'

Wendy laughed. It hurt like hell, but she didn't mind.

'I'd offer you a glass of wine, but I don't think you deserve one after that,' she said, sitting down.

'There are a lot of things I don't deserve,' Xav said, bowing his head. 'Listen, I overreacted before. I know the job's horrendous and that it's always going to get in the way. Policing and relationships don't mix. I know that. But sometimes things are worth trying extra hard for, don't you think?'

Wendy had to agree.

'Listen. Wendy. I'm sorry. I've been thinking a lot over the past few weeks. I know I need to be a lot more accepting of the fact that your job's going to get in the way. I'm going to have to be patient. And I don't mind that. Some things are worth waiting for.'

Wendy looked at him and smiled.

Jack Culverhouse closed the front door behind him and let out a huge sigh. Work had been hell for the past three weeks or so, with the team being two officers down at a time when they were trying to tie up the loose ends and prepare the materials on Operation Mandible for the Crown Prosecution Service.

A fantastic waft of aromas hit him square in the face as he headed towards the kitchen. Emily was standing in front of the stove, stirring a saucepan.

'What's this?' he said, putting a hand on her shoulder.

'I wanted to cook for you,' his daughter said. 'Thought you might like it.'

'Looks like beef stroganoff,' he said. His favourite meal.

'It is. I found a recipe online. Thought I'd have a go. Does it smell okay?'

He smiled. 'It smells beautiful, darling.'

'Good. Now, pour yourself a glass of wine and sit down.'

He was confused. His daughter certainly had her kind moments, but this wasn't like her at all. As she reached to grab a bowl from the sideboard, he noticed some marks on the inside of her forearm as her top rode up her arm, only to be quickly pulled back down again. They looked to him very much like cuts.

'What's going on?' he said.

Emily looked at him, but seemed to misunderstand his question. 'The case is over, isn't it? You said you were handing it over today.'

'Yes. Yes, all done from our side of things.'

There were a number of things still left unanswered, as far as he was concerned. That was often the way following an investigation. It was difficult to separate the lies from the truths and to understand exactly why someone would commit such a crime, but that was down to the courts and the newspapers to decide. His job was to gather enough evidence to be able to charge. As far as he was concerned, he'd done his bit. The rest would all come out in the wash.

'Good. You can relax then, can't you?' she said, pouring a glass of chilled sauvignon blanc into his glass. 'Can I have some?'

'Em, you're not even fourteen.'

'So? It's not illegal. I didn't buy it. I'm under adult supervision. And I'm in my own home.'

He looked at the wine, then at Emily, and smiled. He didn't think she'd ever referred to it as *home* before. She'd lived here as a child before her mother had taken her away, so he guessed technically it was her home. But hearing her say it immediately lifted all his worries. For now, at least.

'Go on,' he said. 'A small drop.'

MORE BOOKS BY ADAM CROFT

RUTLAND CRIME SERIES

1. What Lies Beneath
2. On Borrowed Time
3. In Cold Blood

KNIGHT & CULVERHOUSE CRIME THRILLERS

1. Too Close for Comfort
2. Guilty as Sin
3. Jack Be Nimble
4. Rough Justice
5. In Too Deep
6. In The Name of the Father
7. With A Vengeance
8. Dead & Buried
9. In Too Deep
10. Snakes & Ladders

PSYCHOLOGICAL THRILLERS

- Her Last Tomorrow

- Only The Truth
- In Her Image
- Tell Me I'm Wrong
- The Perfect Lie
- Closer To You

KEMPSTON HARDWICK MYSTERIES

1. Exit Stage Left
2. The Westerlea House Mystery
3. Death Under the Sun
4. The Thirteenth Room
5. The Wrong Man

All titles are available to order from all good book shops.

Signed and personalised books available at adamcroft.net/shop

EBOOK-ONLY SHORT STORIES

- Gone
- The Harder They Fall
- Love You To Death
- The Defender

To find out more, visit adamcroft.net

GET MORE OF MY BOOKS FREE!

Thank you for reading *With a Vengeance*. I hope it was as much fun for you as it was for me writing it.

To say thank you, I'd like to give you some of my books and short stories for FREE. Read on to get yours...

If you enjoyed the book, please do leave a review online. Reviews mean an awful lot to writers and they help us to find new readers more than almost anything else. It would be very much appreciated.

I love hearing from my readers, too, so please do feel free to get in touch with me. You can contact me via my website, on Twitter @adamcroft and you can join my Facebook Readers Group at http://www.facebook.com/groups/adamcroft.

Last of all, but certainly not least, I'd like to let you know that members of my email club have access to FREE, exclusive books and short

stories which aren't available anywhere else. There's a whole lot more, too, so please join the club (for free!) at https://www.adamcroft.net/vip-club

For more information, visit my website: adamcroft.net

Knight & Culverhouse return in

DEAD & BURIED

OUT NOW

Two dead bodies. A corrupt trafficking ring. A betrayal that'll shake Mildenheath to the core.

Two dead bodies are found buried beneath undergrowth just outside Mildenheath. The race is on to uncover their identities and catch their killers.

When two young men tell police they've escaped with their lives from a local brothel where they were kept as male prostitutes, DCI Jack Culverhouse and DS Wendy Knight are left facing a case like no other before.

But as their investigation into the people traffickers and kidnappers gets deeper, they realise the ringleaders will stop at nothing to evade justice.

Turn the page to read the first chapter...

DEAD & BURIED

CHAPTER 1

Zoran Petrovic and Milan Nikolic tried to shelter themselves from the cold as they waited for their pick-up.

Milan had dreamed of living in England ever since he was a boy. He'd spend hours a week back in his home village of Ralja, just south of Belgrade, watching dubbed versions of British dramas. He adored the scenery, loved the customs and traditions. So far, he'd seen none of that.

The man who'd introduced himself as Alexei promised them shelter, accommodation and the start of a new life in England. It wasn't every day you got an offer like that, and Zoran and Milan had jumped at the chance.

Their drivers were delayed, Alexei said. They'd be here as soon as they could, but they had some business to take care of first. Milan had tried to break the interminable silence by asking more about what the work entailed, but Alexei had been vague. All he'd told them was that it was in the hospitality industry.

Alexei was Russian — Milan was fairly sure of that — and he knew that Russians could sometimes be a little abrupt and would only give vague responses. Milan didn't mind too much. He was just pleased to have landed on his feet with a job. He wasn't bothered what job it was. He'd wash pots and pans in a hotel kitchen if he had to. He'd go out in all weathers picking strawberries if it meant he had a chance to make a better life for himself. It was finally starting to come together, and he couldn't wait.

'Where is the work?' Milan asked, speaking to Alexei in English. It seemed to be the only common language they had, although Alexei's English wasn't great. 'Is it in a town or city?'

Alexei took a drag on his cigarette, looked at Milan and blew the smoke out through his nostrils.

'Yes. Town.'

Milan nodded. 'What is the town called?'

'Small town,' Alexei said.

'Yes. What is the name of the town?'

Alexei curled his nostrils slightly and stubbed his cigarette out on the brick wall behind him before speaking.

'Mildenheath.'